The Well of Truth

The Well of Truth

Stories of Spirit

Elizabeth A. Gould

Published by SparkPress, a BookSparks imprint,
A division of SparkPoint Studio, LLC
Phoenix, Arizona, USA, 85007
www.gosparkpress.com

Published 2022
Printed in the United States of America
Print ISBN: 978-1-68463-139-1
E-ISBN: 978-1-68463-140-7
Library of Congress Control Number: 2021920996

Book Design by Stacey Aaronson

For Molly

CHANGE

Said the sun to the moon,
You cannot stay.
Change
Says the moon to the waters,
All is flowing.
Change
Says the fields to the grass,
Seed-time and harvest,
Chaff and grain.
You must change,
Said the worm to the bud,
Though not to a rose,
Petals fade
That wings may rise
Borne on the wind.
You are changing
said death to the maiden, your wan face
To memory, to beauty.
Are you ready to change?
Says the thought to the heart, to let her pass
All your life long
For the unknown, the unborn
In the alchemy
Of the world's dream?
You will change,
says the stars to the sun,
Says the night to the stars.

—Kathleen Raine, "Change"

Contents

The Well | 1

The Wedding Crasher | 7

Eclipse | 13

The Dare | 19

The Uncertainty Principle | 25

Flat White | 32

Mother's Nature | 37

The Home Fire | 41

The Present | 45

Goddess *in the* Closet | 51

Stormy Weather | 56

The Heart *of the* Volcano | 61

Burning Down *the* House | 68

Call *of the* Wild | 71

Demeter's Workout | 77

Pomegranate Season | 80

Eternally Yours, Roma | 83

Godspeed | 87

Quan Yin Comes *to* Dinner | 91

Un Coeur Ouvert (An Open Heart) | 96

Mighty Aphrodite | 111

Taking Off *the* Wetsuit | 117

Out *on a* Limb | 123

Into *the* Fog | 128

The Well

MUD SQUELCHED BENEATH GRACE'S RUBBER BOOTS AS she climbed the rain-soaked hillside. Not wanting to slip and fall, she stepped gingerly around the sheep droppings that littered the footpath. In her head she replayed the conversation she'd just had with a local farmer.

"Excuse me," she'd asked politely, "Do you know the way to the Well of Truth?"

The man tipped his tweed cap and pointed a tobacco-stained finger to the west. "Aye, lassie. Gae doon th' wee path ower th' burn tae th' brae. Ye cannae miss it."

Struggling to understand his dialect, Grace smiled and waved as she headed in the general direction he'd suggested. She strode across the green turf, exuding a confidence that belied the self-doubt she felt inside. *What the hell am I doing in a wet field on a remote Scottish island?*

After graduating from college, many of her friends had moved to New York for high-powered jobs in banking and the corporate sector. Though she'd been happy to pursue an art history degree, studying Italian painting and sculpture instead of accounting or economics, it wasn't easy finding a job, especially a paying one. She decided to postpone the job search in favor of a summer spent traveling in Scotland. With the money she had saved up she would meander through picturesque villages and country lanes, while working on her photography portfolio and researching her Celtic ancestry.

With a plane ticket to Glasgow in one hand and a suitcase crammed with romantic notions in the other, she set off for the mystical land of her forebears. Her heart bore an inchoate yearning to know where she came from in the hope that this might inform her about who she was and what she might become.

Had it not been for her college roommate Barbara, Grace probably would never have found herself in the Outer Hebrides. One evening during their last semester at school, they watched *My Dinner with Andre*. Barbara, an aspiring chef, wandered out of the room when she realized the movie had nothing to do with cooking. But Grace remained riveted by the on-screen conversation between two friends as they talked about a spiritual community in Scotland.

The next morning, over scrambled eggs and toast, Grace confided to Barbara that she planned to visit that place on her summer travels.

"But, Gracie," Barbara exclaimed, "what if it's a cult and they force you to drink the Kool-Aid? We'll never see you again!"

Undeterred, Grace arrived in Glasgow at the end of June, when the golden days of summer lasted well into the evening. Within a week, she had joined a residence program at the community's farmstead on a small island off the coast. Although she was a city girl, it didn't take long for her to get acclimated to the rhythms of rural life:

- Sunrise meditation, followed by tea and porridge
- Morning kitchen duty, chopping vegetables and making bread
- Community lunch at noon
- Wool carding and spinning
- Afternoon tea at three o'clock

On her own until dinner at eight, she got in the habit of taking long afternoon walks. Even though the island was only a few miles long and wide, it revealed itself slowly. By the end of her second week, Grace had clomped through peat bogs and paddocks filled with Highland cattle, seen the white sandy bays in the north and the sheer cliffs of the south. She'd sat in sea caves and found stone cairns in unexpected places. She lost track of time when she was out on the land, which meant that she was often late for dinner. Instead of being annoyed, the other residents were amused when she burst through the back door, ruddy-cheeked and breathless, bringing tales of double rainbows and frolicking seals.

One blustery afternoon, as darts of rain jabbed at the farmhouse window, Grace sat by the peat fire learning how to use a spinning wheel. Her frustration grew as she attempted to treadle and draft at the same time. The local woman teaching her how to spin offered encouraging words: "Don't overthink it. You've got to *feel* your way into the flow."

Grace groaned.

"Let's take a break," the woman suggested. Sensing Grace's distress, she deftly changed the subject. "I hear you've been out rambling across the island. Have ye come across the Well of Truth?"

"I've never heard of it," said Grace.

With a twinkle in her eye, the woman said, "In the old days, the local people would go to healing wells that were said to be the sacred domain of the goddess. But with the passing of time, people forgot about the ancient ways, and the holy wells fell into neglect." Lowering her voice slightly, the woman confided, "There's one here on the island we call the Well of Truth. It's not far as the crow flies, though there are no signs leading to it."

Seeing Grace's eyes light up, the woman continued, "If you follow the dry-stone wall behind the old kirk, it will take you through a pasture. When you cross the stile, you'll find a footpath leading into the hills. The well is at the top." Then, with an impish grin on her face, the woman added, "It is said that the reflection will reveal something about your true self. I'd be curious to know what you see when you look inside."

When the rain stopped that afternoon, Grace went in search of the holy well. Somewhere along the way, she took a wrong turn and ended up at the front door of a small, lime-washed cottage. She knocked lightly and waited, breathing in the perfume coming from the pots of yellow and purple violets that flanked the threshold. An elderly farmer appeared, his eyes rheumy with age. With his thick Scottish accent, he set Grace back on course by pointing to a green mound in the distance that was as gentle and round as a woman's breast.

Midway up the sodden hillock, she stopped to catch her breath. Inspecting her mud-splattered boots and jeans, she smiled with mischievous delight. The natural world was refreshingly straightforward—earth, grass, wind, rock—a welcome reprieve from the heady academic work that had consumed her in college.

Spurred on by the promise of the well's revelation, she continued up the steep path.

Over the rise of the hill, she was rewarded with a panoramic view of the wild Atlantic. Rocky outcroppings, fringed by churning white waves, pocked the surface of the vast ocean. In the distance, a slanting gray sheet of rain stretched from the brooding sky to the bottle-green sea. Around her, the hills formed a vibrant patchwork of purple heather and golden gorse. No matter where she looked, she could see no sign of the human hand—not a car, a ship, or even a cowshed. There were none of the manicured lawns and well-behaved hedges she had grown up with in California. Though it was like no place she had ever known, standing on top of that hill felt like a homecoming. With Nature's wild energy coursing through her veins, she had never felt more alive.

Then, remembering the purpose of her outing, she spun around, looking for the sacred well. She searched among the mossy rocks and tufts of wild irises but couldn't find it anywhere. Looking past a lichen-encrusted boulder, she spotted a sturdy rowan tree, its branches festooned with small strips of cloth. Beneath the tree was a large puddle framed by smooth, white stones. She had found the Well of Truth!

Her body thrummed with excitement as she knelt, wondering what truth the ancient goddess would reveal to her. The moment she touched the cold stones, she trembled, suddenly afraid of what she might see. She peered over the edge of the pool but did not find her image mirrored back to her. Mystified, she leaned in further, searching in vain for her reflection. On the shining surface of the water, a silvery crescent of moon floated, its presence interrupted at times by passing clouds and birds. A gentle wind crooned through the branches of the rowan tree, "This is who you are."

The Wedding Crasher

LIKE MANY BRIDES IN ANTICIPATION OF "THE BIG DAY," Grace hadn't slept well the night before the wedding. Jittery and unable to settle, she wondered if she'd been served regular instead of decaf coffee at the rehearsal dinner. She lay in bed taking deep breaths, a calming technique she had once learned in a yoga class, but it didn't seem to be helping. Through the ruffled curtains of her childhood bedroom, she watched a star move slowly across the sky behind the silhouette of a sycamore tree. The star and the tree were her stalwart companions as she held vigil, waiting for the sun to rise.

When the sky brightened from cobalt to azure to periwinkle, she slowly got out of bed. *This is the last time I'll wake up alone . . . for the rest of my life.* The thought made her heart sink. Had she made the right decision to accept Jack's proposal of marriage? Needing time to think, she put on her running shoes and stepped out into the burgeoning day.

Her feet guided her to the place she had long considered her secret refuge. The front gate of the botanical garden was ajar, giving her entry into a riotous wonderland of fragrance and color. Walking beneath the row of jacaranda trees that dissolved in a blur of luscious purple blossoms, she marveled at the blue agapanthus that nodded their flowering heads as she passed. She touched the trunks of the exotic trees lining the path, calling each one by name: dawn redwood, Surinam powderpuff, Brazilian pepper.

In the perfection of that fine May morning, she swelled with appreciation for her hometown, the City of the Angels. Feeling the warm rays of sunlight on her back, she veered off the trail toward an elegant gum tree perched on a grassy knoll. She sat underneath her favorite tree, her body immediately relaxing, though her mind was still disturbed. *Why am I feeling so miserable on the happiest day of my life?*

The man she was about to wed was brilliant and ambitious, a free spirit with an enormous appetite for adventure. Life with Jack was fun, but was that enough of a reason to get married? Her heart thudded in her chest, knowing that tying the knot was a gamble, possibly the biggest one she would ever take. It didn't necessarily mean that Jack would forsake his carousing ways. *If I want out, this is my last chance.*

Feeling lightheaded, she wrapped her arms around the tree, and whispered beseechingly, "Help me. I don't know what to do."

Throughout her life, the company of trees had soothed and comforted her in moments of necessity. With her cheek pressed against the bark, she felt a pleasant, warm sensation, like liquid gold pouring down over her head, sliding down her arms and legs, connecting her to the earth below. Transfixed, she hugged the tree even tighter, grateful for the generous blessing when she needed it most.

"I wish you could be there at the wedding." she said, looking up into its branches.

Just then, a groundskeeper came stomping down the path in heavy work boots, interrupting her communion with the tree. Grace stood up, a sheepish expression on her face, and moved swiftly toward the front gate. She was ready to face the day.

In the rush of preparations for the wedding, her apprehensions disappeared until she was en route to the church. It didn't help that the stays in her corset dug into her ribs, making it painful to breathe. Her sister, Maureen, sat beside her, offering mints, lip gloss, a sip of water. Anxious and irritated, Grace snapped at her in a tone harsher than intended.

"I don't need anything!"

Embarrassed by her outburst, Grace turned her face to the window. *What is wrong with me?*

When the car stopped at a red light, she was seized with the desire to kick off her satin heels and run barefoot across Wilshire Boulevard. She would flag down the approaching bus and ride it all the way to the airport, where she'd catch the first flight to Glasgow.

Maureen asked, "Gracie, are you OK?"

"Yeah, I just need some time to think."

When the light turned green, Grace wondered aloud why she was thinking about Scotland. Her sister patted her hand reassuringly, saying "You've got wedding day jitters. It's completely normal."

At the church, Grace's father was waiting for his daughters to arrive. When he saw Grace's pale complexion, he swiftly escorted her into the vestibule. "Don't worry, sweetheart," he coached. "Just take this one step at a time."

She clung to his arm as they walked together down the aisle, not sure if she wanted to laugh or cry. Everyone she knew and loved was assembled in the pews: family, childhood friends, college pals, coworkers, and neighbors. Filled with hopeful anticipation, their eyes propelled her toward the altar where Jack, freshly scrubbed in his new suit, stood waiting. When Jack reached out to take her hand, her body flooded with adrenaline and euphoria. *I am getting married!*

After the ceremony, the newlyweds hopped into a waiting limousine. Opening a bottle of champagne, they giddily took their first sip of married life. Grace lowered the tinted window and pointed out that both the moon and sun were visible in the sky, which seemed to her an auspicious omen.

Decked with green swags and twinkling lights, the reception hall had been transformed into an enchanted forest. Grace stood at the threshold of the room, sensing the magic in the air.

After dinner, the ethereal mood vanished when the Irish band took the stage, and the dance floor became a wild, whiskey-fueled crush of jigging bodies. Grace watched in amusement as her new husband cavorted across the dance floor, swigging from a bottle of beer. Surrounded by his inebriated buddies, Jack was in his element. He beckoned her to dance, but she demurred, not quite ready to join the bacchanalia.

In husky voices tinged with alcohol, Jack's friends began to chant, "Come on, come on!"

Grace stiffened, wondering if being married meant that she was expected to do everything her husband wanted. To appease the unruly bunch, she moved toward the dance floor. But just before her foot touched down on the parquet floor, a pair of arms grabbed her around the waist and yanked her backwards. Caught by surprise, Grace spun around, coming face to face with a slender young woman in a green gown.

"Wait a second!" the woman chided playfully. "I'd like to have a word with you."

Perplexed, Grace looked at the rosy-cheeked stranger whose eyes sparkled like sunlight on water, and who gave off the scent of sweet earth.

How do I know her?

Mayhem erupted on the dance floor as the band played at a fever pitch, but Grace, captivated by the mysterious woman, was oblivious to it all.

"As you begin this new phase of your life," the woman said, "remember to stay close to the trees and the flowers, the tides, the moon, and the land around you. They will lead you back to your own true nature."

The lilt of the woman's voice was comforting and vaguely familiar.

How do I know her?

The woman placed her hand lightly on Grace's bodice. "The wisdom of your heart will guide you if you can learn to trust yourself," she continued. "That way, you will never get lost."

Grace could feel her face crumpling. She did not want to hear about getting lost on the day she got married.

"Stay true!" the woman repeated emphatically before vanishing into the boisterous crowd.

Standing at the edge of the dance floor, Grace wanted to ignore the cryptic message. Even so, on some deep level, she recognized the wisdom of these words all too well.

Eclipse

GRACE SAT ON THE CORNER OF SIXTH AVENUE AND Christopher Street with her eyes fixed on the sky. Though it was well past midnight on a bitter cold night, the city was alive with honking, jostling cabs, and the sidewalks congested with people migrating from bars and restaurants. The man sitting in the newspaper kiosk glowered suspiciously at her, but she was not going to let his disapproving looks or the weather distract her from her mission.

Shortly after getting married, Grace and Jack relocated to New York City for his work, landing in a small apartment in the West Village. When she went back to school to get her teaching degree, she signed up to take an astronomy class. She had always been intrigued by the subject, even if a disparaging high school teacher had once told her she had no aptitude for science. Though she'd carried that judgement into her adult life, where she consistently avoided anything related to science or mathematics, her desire to learn about the night sky had become stronger than her fear of failure.

Every window in their tiny apartment looked out on an air shaft, making it impossible for Grace to do her skygazing homework from home. On a nightly basis, she prowled like a wolf around the neighborhood, searching for an open piece of sky. Her assignment that winter night was to watch a full lunar eclipse from start to finish, so she dressed herself in layers of ski clothes before settling down on the steps of the Jefferson Market Library. She pulled her notebook out of her purse, thinking about that first day of class.

Wearing a Harris tweed jacket, Professor Davidson cut an imposing figure as he stood at the podium, surveying the crowded auditorium. With his first words, uttered in a thick Scottish burr, he posed a question: "What is the moon made of, and why does it shine?"

Not certain of the answer, Grace doodled intently in the margins of her notebook. All around her, throats cleared, and feet shuffled. Professor Davidson stood frozen at the lectern, his ear cocked to one side, waiting. After several moments of awkward silence, he muttered *sotto voce*, "This . . . is . . . a . . . problem."

He launched into a dramatic soliloquy that had every student sitting at the edge of their seat.

"The time has come for each of you to reclaim your birthright!" he announced. (Grace wrote those words in bold across the front page of her notebook.) "Every human being is entitled to know the secrets of the celestial rhythms. From this moment on, you will need to watch the sky like detectives. You must take notes, make sketches, record your observations. In this way, you will come to understand the great cosmic mysteries."

Professor Davidson's speech was thrilling, but each time he used a technical word like apogee or azimuth, Grace felt uneasy. That she did not know the meaning of these words only seemed to reinforce her belief that she had no talent for science. How could she reclaim her birthright if she didn't possess the intellectual ability to understand it? She held onto the armrests of her chair, fighting the impulse to get up and leave. Suddenly she was back in high school, reliving that terrible day when she was learning about universal gravitation in science class. She had asked a question about the effect of gravity on the moon, accidentally using the pronoun *she* instead of *it* when referring to the heavenly body. Her teacher, a consummate scientist, sneered at her choice of words, reminding her in front of the entire class that they were studying *science*, not poetry. The boys at the back of the room sniggered, calling her "moon girl" for the rest of the year.

Though she felt mortified at the time, it *was* true that Grace felt a personal affinity with the moon. One of her most treasured childhood memories was of a cool, autumn evening on the way home from dinner at Grandma's house. Sitting in the backseat of the family's wood-paneled station wagon, she'd made an astonishing discovery. The golden harvest moon had followed the car across town, even as it turned corners and stopped at red lights. When the car pulled into the driveway, she was amazed to find the moon shining down benevolently on the roof of her house. *The moon knows where I live!*

Having learned about Greek mythology in school, Grace imagined that Artemis, the maiden goddess of the moon, was her secret friend and confidante. Together they ran barefoot down the beach and climbed oak trees in the park. Artemis taught Grace many wonderful things, including how to talk to animals and the proper way to catch moonbeams in a bowl of water.

When Grace entered high school, she realized that her friends were more interested in boys and parties than in stargazing or Greek goddesses. Begrudgingly, she distanced herself from Artemis, though whenever she glimpsed the moon in the sky, she always sent a covert greeting.

A cyclist singing "Roxanne" at the top of his lungs zoomed down Sixth Avenue, jolting Grace out of her reverie. She remembered that Professor Davidson said the word *lunatic* came from *luna,* Latin for moon, because the ancients believed the full moon had the power to make people go crazy. Just then, a taxicab veered over to the curb in front of her. She recoiled as a young Wall Street type vomited out the rear window, causing her to wonder what Jack and his buddies were up to that evening.

Between the chaos on the streets and the drama in the sky, Grace was thoroughly entertained, though her bones ached with cold. She watched the full moon diminish until it was completely enveloped in shadow, at which point it turned the color of rust. Though the so-called "blood moon" was spooky in both name and affect, she knew it was a phenomenon called Rayleigh scattering, which occurred when air molecules from the earth's atmosphere scattered out most of the blue light so that the remaining light cast a red glow on the moon's surface.

She jotted down some of her observations, realizing as she wrote that her connection to the moon could be both soulful *and* intellectual. The knowledge of science enhanced her intuitive experience, creating a wider lens for her continuing conversation with Artemis.

When a tiny portion of moonlight escaped from the other side of the umbral shadow, she stood up abruptly, waving her arms in the air.

"Look, look!" she gestured to passersby. "The light is returning."

People on the street avoided making eye contact with her, assuming that she was out of her mind. (Why else would a woman in ski clothes be loitering outside on a cold winter night?) The news vendor, clearly embarrassed for her, turned his attention back to his portable TV.

Can't they see what's taking place in the sky?

IT WAS THREE in the morning when she headed back to the apartment. The moon slumped wearily behind a water tower, like a helium balloon with a slow leak. Grace hurried past the Korean deli, the shoe repair shop, the dry cleaners on her way home, her warm bed the only thing on her mind. When she arrived at her building, she noticed a beam of silvery light shining down on the front stoop. Even after all those years, the moon still knew where she lived.

The Dare

GRAVEL CRUNCHED NOISILY BENEATH THE CAR WHEELS as Grace drove down the dark country road. Silhouettes of twisted vines and brooding hills lurked beyond the reach of her headlights, adding to her fear of getting lost at night in the middle of nowhere. She was about to turn around and go home when a tepee, glowing golden on the hillside, came into view. Taking her foot off the gas pedal, she slowed down to get a better look.

The handful of cars lining the shoulder of the road indicated that she was in the right place. She parked the car and stepped out into the night. A smiling crescent moon hung low in the sky, a faint trace of light illuminating its shadowed part. "Earthshine," she said out loud to herself, having learned in astronomy class the scientific name for sunlight reflecting off the earth's surface back onto the moon.

A small lantern on top of a wooden pole marked the path to the tepee. Though her flashlight flickered, about to run out of battery, Grace was glad to have it as she walked up the trail.

It had only been a few months since she and Jack moved back to California, where they were actively looking to buy a house, put down roots, and start a family. Recently, she'd seen a colorful flyer on the bulletin board at the local health food store advertising a women's gathering in a tepee. Being new to town, she was eager to make friends.

A TRILL OF women's laughter tumbled down the darkened hillside. Grace stopped in her tracks, her confidence quickly evaporating. What were they laughing about? What would she do if she found herself inside a tepee full of mean girls?

A shadowy figure stepped out of the darkness. "Don't be afraid," the gentle voice crooned. "I'm going to smudge you before you enter into sacred space."

Grace stood still, her heart still beating wildly as she was enveloped in the earthy smell of burning sage. After that, she was instructed to crawl into the round hole on the side of the tepee. *I'm climbing back into the womb.* On the inside, the women sitting on sheepskin rugs around a warm fire made space for her in the circle. Grace looked around furtively, her attention drawn to a woman with long, gray braids who was tapping on a frame drum with short, wrinkled fingers. The drumming got louder and more insistent. The women in the circle became quiet and closed their eyes. Taking a cue from the others, Grace closed hers too.

Someone began to sing.

"Sacred Corn Mother, come to me.

Make my way sacred, fill me with beauty."

The voice was astonishing—clear and pure, like that of a young girl. Surreptitiously, Grace opened her eyes to see who was singing. What she saw made her shiver, even though she was sitting inches away from the fire. The older woman who played the drum had shape-shifted into a beautiful maiden with dark, plaited hair. Her skin was dewy and bright, and she wore a necklace of berries and blossoms over her intricately embroidered dress.

The maiden looked directly at Grace, inviting her to sing along with the other women. But Grace shook her head apologetically. *I'm new here, and I don't know this song. Besides, I'm not a good singer.* Fierceness flickered in the maiden's dark eyes as if to say, *I dare you to take a risk and let yourself go*!

With that prompting, Grace opened her mouth and began to sing. Before she knew what was happening, she was on a flying carpet of sound, exhilarated by the rising and falling harmonies that floated around her. While she soared through indescribably beautiful landscapes of color and light, she felt herself expand and dissolve, her voice weaving seamlessly into the fabric of the music. It was then she understood that her singing was no better or worse than anyone else's; it was simply a part of the shared song.

A warm drop landed on her hand, followed by another. She wiped away the tears that cascaded down her cheeks.

Why am I crying? I'm not sad; if anything, I feel inexplicable joy! When the singing eventually died down, the women sat in silence, letting the reverberations of sound settle deep into their bones.

Grace noticed that the maiden had changed back into the old woman who, setting down the drum and picking up a gnarled piece of wood, explained to the circle that whoever held the talking stick had the right to speak. Grace squirmed in her seat, wondering what she would say when her turn came.

The woman who had smudged Grace at the entrance to the tepee burst into tears the moment the stick was placed in her hands. She shared with the others her pain over the breakup of her marriage. Unused to such sensitive disclosure, especially from a stranger, Grace fixed her eyes on the fire.

The stick passed to a middle-aged lady in a frilly pink blouse, who announced dramatically that she was having a hot flash. Grace had never heard anyone speak openly about menopause, let alone make a joke about it. But she hung on every word, like an eavesdropper listening in on a forbidden conversation. Then the stick was passed to a young mother, who, exhausted by caring for a sick child, spoke of her resentment of her unsupportive husband. Another woman mentioned that she was menstruating, and then spoke about how her cycle was aligned with the lunar phases. Grace listened carefully, never having considered the connection between her menstrual cycle and the moon.

Finally, the talking stick arrived in Grace's hands. She looked around at the expectant faces radiant in the fire light, unsure of what to say. "As a child," she stammered, "I was taught not to air my dirty laundry. But as I listen to each of you, I see the value of sharing our difficulties. A few hours ago, you were all strangers to me, but now I feel connected to each of you. Somehow, your stories are mine too." The women nodded their heads in agreement.

It was almost midnight when the women disbanded, collecting their coats, and tiptoeing back to their dark houses and sleeping children. Buzzing with energy, Grace decided to stay behind to help clean up. While she gathered empty tea mugs, she turned to the older woman.

"You know," she said hesitantly, "while you were singing, I thought I saw you change into a. . . ." She paused, not wanting to offend. "You looked like a beautiful young girl with flowers in your hair. It was magical."

The old woman's eyes sparkled. "Sitting in sacred space is the place where women can access the many aspects of our nature: the maiden, mother, and the wise one. Sometimes we find things we didn't know were inside of us." Lifting a pitcher of water, poised to douse the fire, she added enigmatically, "The cycles of a woman's life are a wondrous mystery." As she poured water over the flames, a ball of steam unfurled in the air between them, and the tepee went dark.

Though her flashlight was dead, Grace had no problem finding her way back down the hill. When she got to her car, she leaned against the hood, looking up into the dark, velvety sky. Thinking about the profound sense of connection she felt in the tepee, she mused, *That's the way it should be among women. We have so much to learn from each other.* Just then, a shooting star streaked across the sky, trailing a long ribbon of light behind it.

The Uncertainty Principle

AFTER NINE MONTHS OF PLANNING AND PRAYING, GRACE thought she was ready to become a mother. She took prenatal yoga classes, read every baby book she could get her hands on, refinished an old wicker bassinet, and knit a drawer full of tiny sweaters and booties. She was pleased with her doctor and midwife, both of whom would support her desire for a natural childbirth free from medical interventions.

During her third trimester, she joined a birth support group that gathered weekly to watch pregnancy movies and read excerpts from *Spiritual Midwifery*. When new mothers returned to share their birth stories, Grace fantasized about the day she would show off her own healthy baby, extolling the glories of motherhood.

Every afternoon, she sat in her creaky rocking chair looking at the painting of the Tibetan deity Green Tara that hung on the wall. Her yoga teacher had called Tara, "a star that brings forth light," a goddess who guided and protected women in labor. Grace prayed as she rocked back and forth,

"Mother of Liberation, please give me an easy birth." She had done everything right. All that was required now was to wait for the outcome.

As her belly distended and her ankles began to swell, she knew that labor was imminent. The hospital bag was ready by the front door. In addition to a bathrobe, toothbrush, and warm socks, she had packed a bottle of cramp bark tincture and a vial of clary sage oil to ease the pain of the contractions. Inside the front pocket of her duffel, between the amethyst crystal and the relaxing aromatherapy candle, she tucked a list of potential baby names.

The due date came and went, leaving Grace with the fear that she had miscalculated. Her doctor, whose practice aligned with her desire for a natural birth, didn't seem very worried. He told her to come back in a week, hoping that she'd go into labor naturally. When she returned to the doctor's office several days later, she wore an apologetic smile; the baby had not budged.

After testing her amniotic fluid levels, the doctor looked concerned.

"I'm sorry to tell you this, but I'm finding some mild placental abruption that could mean fetal distress. If you don't go into labor this evening, I'm going to admit you to the hospital for an induction. We don't want any complications."

Grace gaped at him, not believing her ears. The doctor, who was supposed to be a champion for natural childbirth, was changing his tune. She returned home from her appointment hell-bent on inducing her own labor: she'd eat spicy food, drink castor oil, try acupuncture, drive down a bumpy road. *Anything.*

The following morning, she waddled into the hospital, clutching a pillow and a mason jar filled with nettle tea. Jack followed behind her, carrying the picture of Green Tara and a bouquet of Naked Lady lilies from the garden. The nurse on duty stifled a laugh when she read Grace's three-page birth plan that included:

- candles in the birthing room
- allowing her husband to cut the umbilical cord (after it stopped throbbing)
- taking home the placenta.

Grace glared at her. *What's so funny?*

After the induction, the contractions began with punishing regularity. Grace could barely catch her breath during the short interval between sets. Her initial excitement about going into labor was now spiked with moments of terror. For all the pain she was enduring, she had barely dilated. The midwife suggested that she get into the tub, hoping that the warm water might relax her muscles, but she preferred to pace back and forth across the floor. Jack sat helplessly in the corner, listening to her bay like a wounded animal.

After several hours of this, Grace began to run out of steam. The midwife, who was running out of patience, took her by the hand and led her to the hospital bed.

"We're going to hook you up to these machines so we can better monitor your progress."

Offended, Grace shot her a look. *You are supposed to be my ally. No drugs, no machines.*

The doctor entered the room a few minutes later, his manner brusque and matter of fact. (Grace hadn't seen this side of him during her prenatal visits.) "We're going to give you an epidural to relax your cervix."

"I don't want one."

"The anesthesiologist will be here in twenty minutes." he replied curtly as he walked out the door, followed by the midwife.

Grace's anger at the doctor turned into shame. *I can't let this happen! How will I be able to face the other women from my childbirth class? Or the yoga teacher, who claimed to have had an orgasmic birth?*

Her thoughts were interrupted by the anesthesiologist, who arrived holding the longest needle she had ever seen. At that moment, she knew her only choice was to surrender control and trust the doctor. Exhausted and defeated, she lay down on the hospital bed.

The epidural took effect immediately, bringing with it a welcome relief from the pain. Paralysis crept swiftly up Grace's legs and torso, stopping just below her collarbone.

The doula checked her cervix. "You're opening beautifully. Already at four centimeters."

Damn, maybe I was wrong to resist the drugs? This makes labor seem like a walk in the park. I'll be fully dilated in no time. Smugly, Grace leaned her head back on the pillow and fell asleep.

She was awakened by loud, beeping noises. Bewildered, she looked around as a team of doctors and nurses rushed into the room.

"The baby's heart rate is dropping. We've got to operate, *now*!"

Petrified, she gripped Jack's hand. "I can't have a caesarean—I didn't read that chapter in the pregnancy book!"

The nurse who lifted her onto the gurney murmured under her breath, "Welcome to parenting, expect the unexpected."

In the harsh, raking light of the operating room, Grace's naked, immobilized body was splayed out, being prepped for surgery. Loud voices echoed in her ears, though she could only see masked faces. Metal tools clanked against a stainless-steel tray. Silent tears fell from her eyes.

This is not how I thought it would be.

"Breathe," the nurse commanded, thrusting an oxygen mask over Grace's nose and mouth. Fighting hard to keep her eyes open, she was aware of a faint pressure on her abdomen. *I can't fall asleep, I'm about to have a baby!* But she was no longer in control. Her eyes wobbled in and out of focus.

How am I supposed to bond with the baby if I can't see properly? The voices in the room got louder; she couldn't decipher whether the sounds were excited or frightened. "Green Tara," she prayed fervently, "deliver me!"

And then she heard a small squeak. *Is that the baby?*

She tried to lift her head, but it was too heavy.

"Is it a boy or a girl?" she asked weakly, the words getting strangled in her throat.

There was no response.

"Somebody tell me, is it a boy or a girl?" she repeated.

Then everything went black.

She woke up in a darkened room.

Did I just have a baby?

Where is everyone?

Have they forgotten about me?

A surge of nausea rose in her throat as she struggled to sit up. Panicked, she realized that she was trapped inside a dead, lifeless body.

In the distance, a tiny seed of light appeared in the darkness. Like a star, it got brighter as it came closer. But Grace's eyes were playing tricks on her; she saw sunbursts, rainbows, and the hazy outline of a winged figure surrounded by a greenish light. *Could this be the angel of death? (Surely women didn't die in childbirth anymore, did they?)*

Then she heard footsteps. . . .

Wait a minute, she thought frantically, *do angels have feet?* Her mind filled with images of all the Italian Renaissance paintings she had ever studied. What about Fra Angelico's *Annunciation*? Or Leonardo's? If they did, she reasoned, they would have been shapely and delicate. Whereas Caravaggio's angels, she knew for certain, had feet with cracked soles and dirty toenails.

The light crept closer.

So much had gone wrong so quickly. Just the other day, she had been sitting in her rocking chair, rubbing her round belly. But now, everything was ruined.

It can't end like this.

With her tongue thick in her mouth, Grace whimpered, trying to say that she was not ready to go, that it was not her time to die.

"Please, let me live," she begged the angel, whose exquisite wings turned into arms, holding something out to her that looked like a lotus flower.

Choking on tears, Grace looked into the eyes of the celestial being.

"Green Tara is that you?" she asked.

The goddess waited patiently for Grace to stop crying before she leaned over and whispered into her ear, "Congratulations. It's a girl."

Flat White

AWAKENED BY THE SOUND OF A RAVEN TAPPING ITS BEAK insistently on the bedroom window, Grace rolled over and grumbled, "Go away! It's too early."

The bird continued to strike forcefully at the glass until it made a hole and climbed through. It hopped onto the bed and pecked at Grace's torso and breasts. Furious, she raised her arm to swat the creature, but when she opened her eyes, there was no bird to be found, only her infant daughter, Skye, waving her tiny fists in the air.

I must have drifted off after the five a.m. feeding.

She looked down at her beautiful baby. At almost four months old, Skye had grown bigger, though she looked so helpless as she flailed around, desperate to nurse. Gently, she pulled the baby closer and placed a nipple into her pink, puckered mouth. Leaning back against the pillow, she listened to Skye take greedy gulps of milk.

On the other side of the king-size bed, Jack was fast asleep. He'd stayed up late again last night. Between his demanding job and her at the beck and call of a hungry baby, it felt like they were strangers who just happened to share a bed. Sometimes Grace wondered if Jack was angry because she didn't dote on him like she used to. Did he resent the time she spent caring for their daughter? Or was it that he no longer found her interesting or attractive? She had no idea.

Mechanically, she picked her sweatpants off the floor where she'd dropped them the night before, steeling herself for a new day. Dawn's rosy glow seeped into the room as she carried the baby over to the changing table. Even in the dim morning light, she could tell that Skye's diaper rash was getting worse. She frowned. *I must be doing something wrong. Or, God forbid, the baby has an incurable disease.*

She dressed Skye swiftly—onesie, leggings, sweater, and booties—before placing her in the baby carrier pouch. This was the daily routine: nurse, change, dress, walk, nurse, change, nap, nurse. Most of the time, Grace cherished the early morning walks she took with her infant daughter, singing songs and telling stories. Sometimes she had fleeting glimpses of Skye's future: skipping across the lawn in a tutu; learning how to ride a bike; posing with her prom date by the plum tree in the front yard.

But that morning, Grace felt raw and unhinged. Everywhere she looked, she saw red. The leaves on the trees. Stop signs. Her own eyes, reflected in a car window. Even the sun was a throbbing magenta ball, washing heaven and earth in a mawkish crimson light. *Red sky in the morning, sailors take warning.*

She felt red inside, too. In her sleep-deprived state, her frustration ran hot, though she didn't know what to do with the anger that bubbled up inside of her. Who could she get mad at? The baby? She was just doing what babies do. And Jack was just doing what Jack did. A sob caught in her throat. Motherhood felt so *hard.*

Skye gnawed on Grace's finger, making a noise that sounded like a grinding motor. *I wonder if she's teething. The book said it wasn't supposed to happen until at least six months.*

Wiping drool onto her sweatpants, she gently admonished her child, "Sweet girl, you've got to give me more than three hours of sleep at night!"

Disheartened, Grace wondered if it was going to be this way until Skye went off to college. The thought filled her with dread, and then she immediately felt guilty for having it.

What she really wanted was coffee, but since she was concerned about how caffeine might affect her breast milk, she'd given it up. Though it had been hard to relinquish, Grace told herself that it was one of the many sacrifices that motherhood demanded. Her thoughts wandered to thinking about how long she should continue to breastfeed, and once again, she felt guilty.

She stepped onto the walking trail that led up to the ridge, noticing a rivulet of dried spit-up on her sleeve. *When I get home, I'll ask Jack to hold the baby so I can take a shower.* She sighed disconsolately thinking of the grocery list and the pile of clothes that needed washing. *Why am I not able to manage any of these simple tasks? What's wrong with me?*

It had become a habit whenever she left the house to check out the other women with young children. She was fascinated by (and a little jealous of) the ones who pushed fancy baby strollers around town, sipping their lattes, it seemed, without a care in the world. How did those women manage to look so put together? Why was she the only one with stains on her clothes?

Caught up in a swirl of negative thoughts, Grace slipped on the loose gravel, and fell hard on the ground. Though the baby was unharmed, she had scraped her palms and ripped a hole in her pants. Trembling, she dusted herself off and continued up the trail.

The hills were shrouded in dark clouds, and a sharp wind blew across the exposed ridge. Fretting that the baby might get cold, Grace pulled Skye's hat down over her ears. She sat down on the wooden bench at the vista point, utterly exhausted. As she bent over to inspect her scraped knee, she noticed something shiny in her peripheral vision. On the ground, next to the bench, was a circle of tiny white pebbles surrounding a tall votive candle bearing the image of the Virgen de Guadalupe. With her gentle brown hands folded in prayer beneath her starry mantle, the Madonna looked serene, even as she balanced gracefully on a crescent moon held aloft by a sturdy angel. Grace leaned in closer to the heat that seemed mysteriously to emanate from the unlit candle. With her voice shaking, she earnestly prayed: "Holy Mother, I'm holding on by a thread here. Please help me."

In that instant, the wind died away, and Grace felt the warmth of a golden light around her. Guadalupe stood before her in a crimson gown, inviting Grace to take refuge under her cloak of starlight that smelled of roses and warm summer nights.

A tender voice rippled through Grace's awareness.

The unconditional love you give to your child, you must give to yourself too. Only when you can love yourself exactly as you are, will you know peace.

If she mothered *herself*, would it make the spit up, the diaper rash, the exhaustion, the distant husband easier to bear?

While she pondered this revelation, a raven landed on the branch of a nearby oak tree, interrupting her thoughts with its loud cawing. But she didn't get annoyed with this bird, like she had with the one that interrupted her sleep. She stopped to admire its inky feathers against the leaden sky until Skye began to protest.

"OK," Grace said to the baby, "Let's go home for a nap. And after that, you and I are going out for coffee."

Mother's Nature

GRACE STOOD OVER THE KITCHEN SINK, BAREFOOT AND pregnant again, doing the breakfast dishes. Knowing that she had become the living embodiment of that unflattering cliché, she shook her head. *This is my life now.*

Though Grace had always wanted to have a family of her own, motherhood was much more demanding that she could have ever imagined. It was a relentless job, requiring late nights and early mornings, seven days a week. Calling in sick wasn't an option. Sometimes she felt bored out of her mind by the repetitive tasks, while at other times she was overwhelmed by the immensity of her responsibilities.

Skye was singing to herself as she sat on her potty chair, which made Grace smile. There was just enough sweetness in the mix to make it all work.

Out of the murky dishwater she fished a small ceramic plate with the words "Cel Ati" written across it. She ran her soapy fingers over the drawing of the pregnant Earth goddess holding a sheaf of wheat, a souvenir she'd gotten from the Etruscan Museum in Rome many years ago. She sighed audibly, thinking about that magical year she'd spent studying in Italy.

In her forays around the Eternal City, she discovered art everywhere—it spilled out of doorways, swayed on clotheslines, and splashed in city fountains. Smitten by Caravaggio's dramatic use of light and Bernini's supple figures, Grace became a regular visitor of Rome's churches and museums. Even though much of the art had religious connotations, the beauty of it touched her soul in a way that religion never had.

After spending a day in the Galleria Doria Pamphilj, she decided to change her major from English to art history. When she called her parents to share the news, there was a meaningful pause on the other end of the phone line. At first, she attributed the silence to a faulty long-distance connection, though when he spoke, her dad's voice sounded strained.

"What are you going to do with an art history degree?"

"Don't worry," Grace assured him, "I've already thought about that. I'm going to minor in photography just to keep my bases covered."

It never occurred to her that her parents might be displeased with her choice. But then again, they were not spending their days like she was, roaming cobblestoned streets, rubbing shoulders with fulminating politicians, stone carvers, and chain-smoking priests. Nor were they drinking espresso, listening to Puccini, and eating gnocchi in rustic trattorias. They had never been to Italy, so how could they understand the effect that these sensual pleasures had on her?

As Grace placed the dish carefully on the drying rack, her eye landed on a faded postcard of Bernini's *Daphne and Apollo* taped on the refrigerator door. The first time she saw the sculpture in the Borghese Gallery, she marveled at the genius it took to make a piece of stone seem so alive. Depicting the moment that Daphne turned herself into a tree to escape the advances of Apollo, the artwork drew her back to the museum on a regular basis to admire the nymph's bark-covered torso and leaf-sprouting fingertips.

Though she loved to sit on the balustrade of the Terrazzo del Pincio overlooking the obelisks and gilded domes of Rome's skyline, she felt most at home among the tranquil, tree-lined paths of the Borghese Gardens. Never in a rush to return to her tiny apartment in Monte Mario, she lingered after school, reading Keats on a park bench, or watching the ducks splashing in the lake at the Temple of Aesculapius. It was here that she felt she could sense, however faintly, the beating heart of the ancient Earth Mother, Cel Ati. The rose-ringed parakeets squawking in the umbrella pines and the tenacious blades of grass sprouting up between the ancient cobblestones were evidence enough for her of Cel's enduring presence.

Grace plunged her hands back into the lukewarm dishwater, thinking about that cold Roman night she wore her winter coat to bed. How surprised she had been the following morning to wake to a preternatural silence, devoid of the usual sounds of sputtering diesel engines and whining mopeds. When she opened the curtains, she discovered that the balconette was covered in snow. Grabbing her camera, she hurried down the hill toward the *centro storico.* Aside from a murmuration of birds filling the sky, the city was quiet and tranquil. The plane trees on either side of the sluggish Tiber were heavy with snow; the cormorants that usually sunned on the riverbanks were nowhere to be seen. Grace plowed through knee-high snowdrifts until she reached Saint Peter's Basilica, where she stood breathless in the middle of the vast piazza. Overnight, Cel had worked a miracle, transforming the noisy, frenetic city into a heavenly landscape.

A swift kick in the ribs rousted Grace out of her fantasy. She pulled the plug out of the sink and let the suds, like her daydream, swirl down the drain. *That was then; this is now.*

With her hand on her protruding belly, she lumbered down the hall to the bathroom where Skye was waiting for her. Grace realized that in her own body, Mother Nature was currently at work creating a masterpiece the world had never seen before.

The Home Fire

GETTING THE CHILDREN TO BED EVERY NIGHT WAS AN exhausting ritual that involved saying prayers, giving foot rubs, back scratches, and telling elaborate, off-the-cuff stories. When the children finally dozed off, their breathing heavy and distant, Grace tiptoed downstairs to turn off the lights and lock the door.

Ever since Jack got promoted at work, his life was dictated by extended business trips to far-flung destinations, where time zone differences made it difficult to stay in touch. Though she did her best to hold down the fort on her own, Grace felt lonely. And burned out.

She wriggled out of her clothes and got into a cold bed. Troubling thoughts swarmed in her mind:

What should I do about the blinking warning light in the car?

The black mold on the windowsill?

My mother's upcoming hysterectomy?

Starving polar bears stranded on melting ice caps?

She flopped from side to side, unable to find a comfortable position. She needed someone beside her whispering assurances that everything would be all right. *Damn Jack! What's the use of having a husband if he's never around?* The bedsheets coiled tightly around her legs, turning into enormous, writhing serpents that threatened to devour her. Thrashing around on the bed, Grace screamed, *"Someone help me!"*

She sat up, feeling adrenaline pulsing madly through her bloodstream. The digital clock on the bedside table flashed a mysterious code 3:33 in red lights. She was a volcano ready to erupt, even though the core of her being felt frozen solid.

In the morning, she crept downstairs to make coffee, her cherished daily ritual. She sat by the window in the quiet house, planning the day. Carpool. Groceries. Swim class. Neighborhood kids over for lunch and crafts. Laundry. Always laundry. Outside her window, the gum trees were ablaze with fiery vermilion blossoms, a reminder that summer was over and that cold, dark days were on the way.

By nightfall, Grace was exhausted. *I don't know how much longer I can keep this up.* Even though her daughters protested, she put them to bed earlier than usual. Lying on the floor of their room, she made up a story about a dragon who forgot how to breathe fire. Before long, the words evaporated in her mouth, and she found herself drifting away to an ancient temple surrounded by alabaster pillars.

"Anyone here?" she called out, her voice echoing through the tomb-like silence. She sat down by the central brazier, which was filled with ashes. After waiting a long time for something to happen, she lay down beside it, resting her cheek on the cool marble floor.

"Mama, Mama!" her daughters squealed when they found Grace asleep on the floor of their room. "You forgot to go to bed!"

Grace was tired and irritable all day. In the late afternoon, as she was folding the laundry, she remembered the dream. Reflexively touching her cheek, she recalled how soothing the marble had felt against her skin.

That night she dreamt of the temple again. She was hiding behind a marble column, watching a priestess in a golden robe carefully remove the ashes from the brazier. With great care, the woman built the fire, layering pine and cedar kindling with oak logs. She blew life into the fire; it sputtered and coughed, producing much smoke but little heat. The woman turned to Grace and said pointedly, "You cannot feed a fire with resentment."

Grace woke up sweating, the words echoing in her head.

Not able to remember the name of the Greek goddess of the hearth, she took a mythology book off the shelf to discover that Hestia was the powerful presence who ruled over the domestic realm. Devoted to family and community, the goddess tended the eternal flame; She was the invisible force that kept the world turning.

For the third night in a row, Grace returned to the

dream temple. This time, she was kneeling beside Hestia at the central brazier, adding handfuls of dried rosemary to the fire. The aromatic flames grew, casting a bright dancing light onto the marble pillars.

"Take care with what you kindle in your heart." Hestia said. "Will your spark provide warmth and illumination, or will it burn down your house?"

Grace woke to the sound of rain falling on the rooftop. It was time to make the first fire of the season. Slipping on her raincoat, she went out to the garden shed, filling her arms with all the firewood she could carry. Having received instruction from Hestia, she knew exactly what to do to keep her fire lit.

The Present

THE HOLIDAY SEASON, WITH ALL THE TIDINGS OF PEACE and goodwill, was Grace's least favorite time of year. She begrudged all the expectations, the perfunctory events, the "making merry" when all she wanted to do was stay home reading by the fire. Two days before Christmas, she got up in the morning while the sky was still studded with stars. She splashed cold water on her face, hoping it would give her the jolt of energy she needed. With exactly twenty-four hours before the family road trip, there was laundry to be done, suitcases to be packed, and homemade gingerbread cookies to be delivered to the neighbors. The dog had to be dropped off at the kennel, and Skye had a piano recital in the early evening.

Having recently decided to jump-start her career as a fine arts photographer, Grace had been thrilled to receive an invite to a Christmas luncheon hosted by an art collector and socialite. Though "the ladies who lunch" had never been her thing, Grace knew that she'd be foolish to turn down this rare opportunity to hobnob with the art world elite.

The fly in the ointment was that she couldn't find a thing to wear. Cursing under her breath, she rummaged frantically through her closet, looking for an appropriate outfit. She was certain that the other women would be wearing smart Chanel suits or designer dresses, but since she owned none of these things, she settled on a nondescript black dress—perfectly serviceable, but boring as hell.

She walked from her car to the hotel, her heels click-clacking in staccato rhythm on the pavement. She hadn't dried her hair properly before she left the house, so she shivered from nervousness and cold as well.

After being greeted by a smiling doorman, she was ushered into a refined world of gilded mirrors and tasseled curtains. The hotel's concierge steered her toward the banquet room, where a group of well-coiffed ladies sat at tables decorated with pine boughs and topiary. The woman who had invited Grace was standing in the middle of the room, offering a toast to truth and beauty. Grace moved inconspicuously to the nearest available seat, where a tuxedoed waiter discreetly appeared at her elbow with a flute of champagne.

Over crab salad and Parmesan flatbread, she chatted with the urbane woman next to her, who had just returned from seeing a Corot exhibit in Paris. Together, they bonded over their mutual love of his sultry landscapes and restrained palette. Every now and then, Grace glanced over toward the kitchen, waiting for dessert to be served so she could make her escape. The waiters moved languidly, while the woman beside her talked incessantly about her trip to France. *Don't these ladies have anything else to do today?* Just as a waiter entered the room holding a coffee pot, Grace excused herself and headed toward the door. A shrill voice called out behind her.

"You can't be leaving just yet!"

Grace cringed. *Busted.*

The hostess, who was fully in her cups, ambled over to her.

"The last to arrive and the first to leave . . . don't you like my little party?" she teased.

Before Grace could demur, the older woman leaned in so close that Grace could smell the seafood on her breath.

"I'd love to hear about the projects you're working on, but I see you're in a rush to get somewhere else." The hostess sniffed. "Well, don't forget to take your party favor—I brought these bath salts back from Kona." With a profusion of thanks, Grace left the room clutching the salts in her sweaty hands, wondering who in the world had time to soak in a bath.

Once outside the building, she noticed the sun hanging low in the sky, which meant it was later than she thought. *I'm screwed.* Pulling her coat tighter around her neck, she hurried down the sidewalk through the long shadows cast by the barren trees. *Why does my life seem like a constant battle against the clock?*

With exactly twenty minutes to get through rush hour traffic to Skye's piano recital, she strapped on her seatbelt and hit the gas.

Feeling guilty and looking disheveled, she arrived late at the auditorium. From the disapproving looks of the other parents, she knew she had missed her daughter's solo. Thinking herself the worst mother in the world, she slumped down into her seat, and within seconds was softly snoring.

At the reception, Grace tried to make amends by offering her daughter a cup of hot cider and a cookie, but Skye rebuffed her efforts. Though they had planned to have a mother–daughter dinner together after the performance, Skye changed her mind and wanted to go home. As they drove through city streets decked out with lights and festive garlands, they did not speak a word to each other.

Back at home, Jack put the girls to bed. Grace retreated to the bedroom, where she fell asleep, fully clothed, on the bed.

A low, rumbling sound jolted her awake. What she feared was an earthquake was only her daughters rolling their plastic suitcases down the hallway. She could hear Jack walking in and out of the front door, his feet stamping impatiently on the doormat as if to say, *we've got to hit the road, or we'll get stuck in traffic.*

Though she wanted nothing more than to stay in bed all day, she lurched into the bathroom, locking the door behind her. Even after a full night's sleep, she felt utterly depleted. She sat on the toilet seat with her head in her hands, feeling sorry for herself.

Hands thumped on the bathroom door.

"Mommy, mommyyyy! Let us in!" When Grace didn't answer right away, the children kicked at the door.

"Just a minute, girls." she said as calmly as she could, "I'll be right out. Please stop banging."

Skye's voice rose above the din. "Mommy, I need to talk to you." Her plea, tinged with a plaintive whine, reminded Grace of her inadequacy as a parent.

"I'll be right out," she repeated. "Have Daddy make you some breakfast."

A shaft of sunlight illuminated Grace's face as she looked in the mirror. Shadows danced across her skin, shifting and softening her features. Purplish hollows appear in her cheeks; she noticed the deep creases of skin that formed around her mouth. Her hair glinted in the light like silvery frost, and then the hoary reflection in the mirror spoke to her.

"It is winter now, when even the sun must rest. You need to slow down. Start right now by taking a bath."

"Are you kidding?" Grace countered, "I've got to hustle out of here."

"Don't you see," the old woman replied, "that when you take care of yourself, everyone benefits?"

"But isn't that selfish of me?"

"Not at all! Give it a try." The ancient voice shattered like ice and melted away.

Grace turned the hot water tap on full bore. She emptied the entire packet of volcanic bath salts into the water and lowered herself into the tub. In the distance she could hear cutlery clanking, which meant that Jack and the girls were eating breakfast. *They have no idea that I'm taking a bath!* Smiling, she slid her head beneath the surface and floated away in timelessness.

When her fingers were sufficiently pruned, she stepped out of the bath, feeling invigorated. She walked into the hallway, almost tripping over Skye, who sat outside the bathroom door.

"Honey, what are you doing here?"

"Mommy," Skye said with urgency, "I have to tell you something! I was mad at you last night because you're always late. But then I had a good idea!" Flashing an innocent smile, she added, "I'm going to ask Santa to bring you some more time, so that you're not always in a rush." Pleased with her solution to the problem, Skye reached out to hug her mother.

Grace gathered her daughter in her arms and showered her with kisses, knowing full well that time is a gift you must learn to give yourself.

Goddess in the Closet

IT WAS LATE AFTERNOON BY THE TIME GRACE FETCHED THE clothes off the line. Though the day was warm and bright, and the garden hummed with life, Grace spent it under a dark cloud of her own making.

That morning, after Jack left for work, and her sister, Maureen took the girls to the zoo, Grace stepped into the shower. Before she knew what was happening, her body collapsed in slow motion to the tiled floor, her salty tears mixing with the warm shower water. Strange, animal noises erupted from her mouth, echoing off the bathroom walls. Images of the night before, when she and Jack were out celebrating their wedding anniversary, flashed through her mind:

Carefully putting her makeup on.

Jack honking the horn impatiently.

Walking to the car, feeling pretty.

Jack on a business call, ignoring her on the drive to the restaurant.

Coquettish waitress with low décolleté flirting with Jack.

Jack flirting back.

Feeling queasy but pretending to enjoy the meal.

Vomiting up the expensive meal in the ladies restroom.

Returning to the table, shaky and sweaty.

ON THE RIDE home, Grace told Jack that he had hurt her feelings.

"You've got to be kidding!" he said, laughing.

"Well, the flirting was really noticeable, at least to me," she replied defensively.

"You need to get a life." he said half-jokingly, though Grace felt the barb in his words.

Did I overreact? Maybe he's right, and I do need to get a life.

The shower water turned cold, but there was heat rising within her.

How dare he flirt so flagrantly in front of me! Are things really that bad between us? She gasped, finally seeing what she had been denying all along—their marriage was falling apart. The rage that overcame her was ferocious, giving her an undeniable boost of energy. Taking a strange pleasure in scrubbing the dirty grouting, she cleaned the hell out of the bathroom. She stormed through the house, knocking the vacuum canister recklessly into the living room furniture, and ripping the sheets off the beds.

I was a fool to think my love could change Jack.

I married the wrong guy.

What do I do now, especially with two daughters to consider?

With her Catholic upbringing, divorce didn't seem like an option. *We'll have to find a good therapist to get us through this.* But why was she feeling bad about herself? As if she had done something wrong, as if she were the one to blame in all of this.

She went into the backyard to pull the clothes off the line, pausing briefly to stick her nose into the clean linen that smelled of sunshine. Lugging the laundry basket up the stairs, she stopped abruptly when she saw a gorgeous stranger, backlit by the sun, standing in her bedroom doorway.

The beautiful woman, wearing a slinky evening gown that had languished in Grace's closet for years, sashayed down the hall, filling the air with the wild and electric sound of bees foraging through a field of lavender. The lady was as radiant and lovely as a summer's day, trailing the fragrance of full-blown roses. When she stepped out the front door, the wind chimes rang exuberantly on the porch. Birds and butterflies gathered overhead to perform elaborate dances in the air.

Standing there in her frumpy sweatpants, Grace could not help comparing herself to this vision of exquisite beauty and grace, who possessed something that she herself desperately craved but could not name. *Was it self-confidence? Erotic energy? Feminine power?*

Outside the garden gate, it became clear that Grace

wasn't the only one in pursuit of the goddess. Men stopped their cars in the middle of the road to gawk; women rushed out of their homes, leaving children unattended and dinner in the oven. People came down off ladders and out of bushes to catch a glimpse of her.

Like drones swarming around the queen bee, they gathered, whispering, "It's Freya, the Queen of Beltane!" Though Grace hadn't the faintest idea what they were talking about, it didn't stop her from wanting to get closer. The crowd followed Freya up a hidden footpath between two houses that led into a dense, dark forest, a place that Grace had never noticed before.

The May Queen led the procession through the woods into a glade where bright flowers sprang up out of the green grass, forming a multicolored carpet. When Freya stepped into the meadow, something unusual happened. Every breath got caught behind teeth and tongue, every heart arrested. Birds paused mid-flight. Even the sun, millions of light years away, tempered its fiery barrage.

The queen's bright eyes skimmed over the crowd of pretty boys and macho men, cool dudes and masters of the universe, who were all competing for her attention. She, however, only had eyes for a partner who was loving and kind.

The crowd waited in hushed anticipation as Freya chose her consort. When the queen reached out her hand to her beloved, the crowd cheered, the wine splashed, and the

Beltane fire roared to life. Someone shouted, "Let the merrymaking begin!"

Grace, quiet as a shadow, followed the lovers as they retreated into the darkening forest. She hid behind the trunk of an tree, taking note of the ways the man showed his adoration of the queen. Grace felt a jab of envy; Jack never looked at *her* like that. Dusk fell gently around the lovers, wrapping them in a cloak of invisibility. Grace fell asleep at the base of the tree, listening contentedly to their sighs and whispers.

The next thing she knew, she was lying on her bed next to the basket of clean clothes. The closet door stood wide open, revealing the beautiful gown, freshly pressed, as if it had never been worn. Untying her ponytail, she let her long hair cascade luxuriantly around her shoulders. "You are beautiful" she murmured to herself, "and I love you just as you are." She ran her fingers through the silky fabric of the dress before she slipped it over her head. Taking in her reflection in the floor-length mirror, she could not deny that the dress fit her perfectly.

Stormy Weather

THE MARRIAGE COUNSELOR SUGGESTED THAT A ROMANTIC getaway would be the best medicine for their relationship. Grace found a rental property on the coast that seemed to fit the bill, a place where she and Jack could relax in the sun and take long walks on the beach. In preparation for their holiday, she shaved her legs, painted her toenails, and even splurged on a silky black nightie. (How was she to know, as she stood in line at the lingerie shop, that it would never be worn?)

The weather forecast didn't look good, but Grace wasn't worried. *Nowhere to go, nothing to do. What could be better?*

But the premature darkness of the sky, which portended a powerful storm, gave her pause. By the time they arrived at the beach house, two things were obvious: the tumble-down cottage looked nothing like it did in the photos, and a vicious tempest was about to hit.

As fat, cold drops of rain began to fall, Grace grabbed the grocery bags and headed inside the house. The kitchen countertops were sticky, and the inside of the silverware drawer was filled with crumbs. She rummaged around until she found the corkscrew. *Put your own oxygen mask on before assisting others.* She downed a glass of pinot noir, savoring the warmth it created as it slid down her throat. Jack, looking through the video cassettes stacked on top of the bookshelf grunted his approval when handed a wine goblet, not bothering to look up at his wife.

We're decompressing, Grace told herself as she walked back into the kitchen to make dinner.

Jack put on an old movie and sprawled on the sofa, leaving no room for her. Unfazed, she settled into the bulky armchair that reeked of cigarette smoke.

They ate dinner in silence, the flickering blue light of the TV screen reflecting on their faces. Grace pulled a crocheted blanket around her shoulders, grateful to be protected from the storm that raged outside. She closed her eyes, imagining that the wind was a wild woman pounding her fists on the corrugated rooftop and knocking over trash cans. Warm and well-fed, Grace drifted off to sleep. In the distance, she thought she heard a voice shrieking, "Stay awake! See what is happening right in front of you!"

Grace woke with a kink in her neck after sleeping all night in the chair. She looked over at Jack, who was snoring on the couch. *We must have been more tired than I thought.*

In the kitchen, she looked through the cabinets for coffee filters. Jack yawned loudly in the living room.

"That was some crazy weather last night." she offered brightly, handing him a cup of instant coffee. "Luckily, the rain is supposed to clear up this afternoon."

Jack didn't respond.

"So, what should we do?" she asked playfully. "I don't know about you, but I haven't played Scrabble in years."

"I've got a headache," Jack announced. "I'm going to bed." Picking up a paperback thriller, he retreated to the bedroom, closing the door behind him.

Grace scraped egg residue out of the frypan, fighting against the impulse to cry. Thunder rolled in the distance as she wandered through the living room to stand outside the closed bedroom door.

"Just checking to see how you're doing. Can I bring you anything?" Grace asked, poking her head into the room.

Jack was sitting in bed with his computer on his lap.

"Nah, I'm fine."

"You hungry? Need an aspirin?"

"No."

"All right then. Get some rest." she said wistfully, shutting the door behind her.

She paused.

This isn't turning out like I expected, thought the crestfallen lover.

It's too bad that Jack's not feeling well, said the inner caretaker.

What if he's avoiding me? asked the angry wife.

You're being paranoid, replied the optimist.

What if my intuition is right? suggested her wise self.

She turned around and went back into the bedroom.

"What's up?" he asked in mild surprise.

"Everything OK with you? I mean, with *us*?"

Jack closed the lid of the computer and gave her an anguished look.

Uh-oh.

"Actually, there *is* something I've been meaning to tell you . . ."

Her heart dropped into her stomach.

(Oh, God.)

"I've met someone."

What???

"And I'm in love with her. I want a divorce."

"You're kidding, right?"

"No," he replied, his mouth twisting up in a grimace. "This is really hard for me."

A hard laugh escaped her lips. "What the hell, Jack! What happened to 'death do us part'? We made a vow to each other, a commitment! Remember that?"

Jack burst into tears. She couldn't recall the last time she had seen him cry.

"I want to be with her, and I just can't keep up the charade any longer."

Although Jack's lips were still moving, she could no longer hear what he was saying. It was as if a swarm of killer bees had filled her head, making it impossible for her to think or see clearly.

Shocked and numb, she staggered out the front door in

the direction of the beach. Rain fell like spittle on her face, and the wind yanked her hair. Standing on the high bluff, she was desperate for a sight of the sea, but a fog bank, thick as death, hung off the shoreline, obscuring the view. Brokenhearted, she stumbled across the dunes, collapsing on the wet sand. She lay there for a long time, finding a primal comfort in the sound of the waves heaving and retreating.

When the rain stopped, the sky lit up like a watercolor painting in dappled coral and mauve light, creating a dramatic backdrop for the upended tree buried in the sand. Looking at its roots dangling helplessly in the air. Grace felt a strong connection to it. Her life, too, had just been turned upside down.

The ferocious storm had at last subsided, leaving behind a gentle breeze that smelled of fresh grass and wildflowers. The soft wind gently combed its fingers through Grace's tangled hair, whispering sweetly, "This too will pass."

The Heart of a Volcano

WHEN GRACE EMERGED FROM THE HOUSE WITH suitcase in hand, the three crows on the telephone wire cackled uproariously. *Are they trying to tell me something, perhaps to warn me of some danger ahead?*

Though it was a sunny, daffodil-scented spring morning, Grace felt anything but light and carefree. She was on her way to the airport to visit her sister, Maureen, in New Zealand. Thanks to her beloved grandmother who had died the previous year, Grace had an unexpected windfall and the resources with which to indulge her love of travel.

The trip had been arranged months ago, but now that Grace was en route, she was having second thoughts. It had barely been a month since Jack dropped the divorce bomb on her. Since then, she'd stumbled around in a daze, stepping back and forth across the border between grief and denial. Over the phone, Maureen helped her pack her suitcase saying, "All you need is a warm sweater, good walking shoes, and a passport."

The truth was that Grace wasn't worried about leaving town, but she *was* petrified about what would happen when she came back. *What does 'home' mean anymore?* Jack would move out, and their little family would never be the same again. As the plane lifted off the ground, she looked out the window, feeling the precariousness of being inside a metal tube hurtling through the sky. *How will I cope?* Stifling a sob, she closed her eyes and tried to sleep.

As the plane descended, Grace looked out the window at the Auckland skyline. The man seated next to her pointed at the volcanic cinder cone rising out of the Hauraki Gulf.

"That's Rangitoto," he said. "It's an easy climb to the summit, and the views at the top are outstanding. You should definitely go there while you're in Auckland."

"As a matter of fact," she replied," I've been wondering what to do on my twenty-four-hour layover."

At dawn the next morning, Grace stood on the wharf, waiting to catch the first boat to Rangitoto Island. Overnight, she had gone from one side of the world to another, from the warmth of spring to the chill of autumn. Feeling seasick before even getting on the boat, she questioned the wisdom of her outing.

But as she stood on deck with sea spray on her face, she felt a tremor of excitement. Once she arrived on Rangitoto Island, she moved swiftly over the pockmarked lava beds to the ascending path, which was much steeper than she anticipated. By the time she reached the top, she was breathing hard. She placed her hands on the rust-colored earth and prayed, "Spirit of the volcano, be with me on this journey."

Then, after a moment of reflecting on the troubles waiting for her back at home, she added, "Teach me how to hold on and how to let go."

On cue, the sun broke through the marine layer, casting a honeyed light over the bay. With a skip in her step, Grace began the descent back to the boat. She stumbled over a rock on the path. Delighted to find that it was heart-shaped and fit comfortably into the palm of her hand, she took it as a good luck talisman for her journey. When she returned to the airport for her flight to the South Island, she reached into her pocket to make sure it was still there.

Maureen met her at the airport with flowers and smiles. "I've got a surprise for you," she said, grabbing Grace's bag. "I'm taking you camping on the most beautiful beach in the world. I've already packed in the car with everything we need," she added, beaming, "including chocolate."

On the winding mountain roads, Grace began to feel nauseous. *It must be the jetlag.* By the time they set up camp on the beach, she had to lie down. She climbed into her sleeping bag, clutching the lava rock. Her temperature alternated between hot and cold, and no matter what position she slept in, her back ached. *Did I pull a muscle lifting my luggage?*

The next morning Maureen brought her a cup of tea. "Wakey, wakey. We've got a beautiful day ahead."

"I'm not feeling well," Grace said.

"Then you need more sleep," Maureen advised.

By midday, Grace was so weak that she could barely stand up. Maureen decided to take her home to rest in a proper bed.

Grace woke up in a dark, unfamiliar room. *How did I get here?* Drenched in sweat, she kicked away the wool blanket that smelled like a wet dog.

A floorboard creaked.

"Who's there?" Grace called out.

A pair of eyes flashed in the darkness. "I am Mahuika, spirit of the volcano."

"What do you want from me?" Grace asked timidly.

"It was *you* who summoned *me*!" the goddess roared. "And *I* want to go home!"

Am I delirious?

Grace tried calling to Maureen, but her throat was dry. "I'm so thirsty," she rasped, "I need something to drink."

Mahuika smiled obligingly, a glass of cold water appearing in her hand. Grace took a large gulp, then spat it out, realizing it was salt water.

"Please," Grace begged, "leave me alone."

"And why couldn't *you* leave *me* alone?!" the goddess retorted angrily, brandishing her red-hot nails.

I must be having a nightmare, but it feels so real.

Grace's body transformed into a lava flow moving slowly through a barren landscape; her mouth was filled with the grit of ashes. And then she was flying across the sky on a hang glider, attached by a row of bungee cords.

"What will you give me in order to be free?" asked the volcano woman.

Grace said the first thing that came to mind. "My expectations."

"Very well," Mahuika replied, "You may detach one cord."

A wave of sweet relief washed over Grace when she unhooked the first cord. But the agonizing heat returned with a vengeance.

"What *else* are you willing to let go of?"

"You can take everything I brought with me: my phone, my clothes, my money."

With that, Grace was allowed to unhook the second bungee cord. Again, she was hit by a momentary gust of cool air.

Now she understood the game: when she let go of something, she found peace, however temporary it might be.

"What will you give me now?" asked the deity in a rising rumble.

"My fears about what will happen when I get home."

She unlatched a third cord. "What *else*?" thundered the volcano goddess like she was about to erupt.

Grace stammered, not prepared to let go of anyone she loved.

"Give it back!" Mahuika fumed.

"I don't know what you want from me," Grace whimpered.

"I want the rock!"

"Take it," she answered feebly.

Now she was falling through the air in slow motion, landing on a bed that smelled of sulfur. She got up and walked out to the garden. In her pajamas, she lay down on the cool, wet ground to listen to the dawn chorus of the tui and bellbirds. Somewhere in the distance, a dog barked, and a tea kettle whistled. The sounds were mundane, yet achingly beautiful to her ears. *The present moment is all there is. This is 'home.'*

Maureen came outside to gently shepherd her sister back into the house. Over breakfast, Grace told her the whole story, from climbing the volcano in Auckland to finding the heart-shaped rock to her nightmarish encounter with Mahuika.

Maureen nodded knowingly. "The Maori say it's *tapu*—forbidden—to remove an object from a sacred site. You've angered the volcano goddess; you must return the rock before you leave."

A week later, on her short layover in Auckland, Grace hailed a cab at the airport terminal. Trying to explain her predicament to the driver, she said, "Take me to the bay, somewhere with a view of Rangitoto Island, and then I will need you to bring me back to the airport to catch my flight." The driver scratched his head, pondering this unusual request.

A quarter of an hour later, the taxi pulled up to a dock in an industrial zone where an old man was fishing.

"Will this do, Miss?"

Grace stepped out of the car, clutching the rock tightly in her hand. "Wait here," she instructed, "I'll only be a minute."

Sunlight sparkled like diamonds on the water as Grace walked to the end of the pier. With her eye on Rangitoto Island in the distance, she hurtled the rock as far as she could into the bay, watching the ripples expand across the surface. Knowing that she had returned the rock to where it belonged, she felt a sense of peace wash over her. Grace stepped into the waiting taxi. She was ready to go home.

Burning Down the House

GRACE LOOKED OUT OVER THE BEACH, WHERE LARGE pieces of driftwood lay scattered like bleached and broken bones. On her way down to the water's edge, she picked her way through glossy ribbons of bladderwrack and decomposing fish carcasses. *Why have I come back here?*

An unexpected gust of wind kicked sand into her face, which felt like a personal affront. She hadn't been back to this beach since the day that Jack asked for a divorce. She spat on the ground. *Why can't I accept that the marriage is over? Why can't I move on?*

With a strong wave of emotions moving through her, she longed for the safety of a sheltered place to sit down and process her thoughts. Remembering that, as a child, she loved making huts out of waterlogged branches, she set to work creating a makeshift refuge. But once she got inside the rickety structure, she was overwhelmed by the scent of damp decay, which only made her feel worse.

With her chin resting on her knees, she closed her eyes to listen to the waves. But what she heard instead was heavy breathing, raspy and asthmatic. Alarmed, she looked up to see a woman marching across the sand toward her. The stranger, who wore a blood-red sari, had kohl-lined eyes and vermilion *sindoor* smeared across her forehead. She waved at Grace and flashed a toothy smile. And then she raised her sinewy arm and knocked down the driftwood hut. Surrounded by the fallen pieces of wood, Grace sat motionless in the sand, transfixed. The fierce woman produced a ball of red yarn from her pocket and began walking in a clockwise circle around Grace, unspooling the wool as she went. Finally, she raised her arms to the sky, invoking the names of Grace's maternal ancestors, "Berthe, Cora, Ellen, Sophie. Lend your courage and strength to break the chain."

Then, with a gleeful chortle, the woman struck a match and lit the ring of fire. Grace shook as an intoxicating fury seeped out of the pores of her skin. While the woman clapped and cheered, Grace raged, slashed, and screamed at all the bitter memories that haunted her, stopping occasionally to vomit up a dark brew of undigested anger. Wilder than the wind and more dangerous than a riptide, she had become a bearer of destruction. *This is it. I am being totally and utterly annihilated.*

The flaming sun crashed flamboyantly into the darkening sea. Grace fell down on the sand. Very slowly, the sea advanced, gathering up her lifeless body in its white, foamy fingers. The tide rocked her in its healing arms until the first light of dawn, when it gently deposited her wet body back on shore.

With saltwater and fire pulsing through her veins, Grace raised her dripping head to thank the wild woman who had saved her life by introducing her to the transformative power of sacred rage.

Call of the Wild

IN THE POLISHED DOORS OF THE ELEVATOR, GRACE STARED at her distorted reflection. Under the fluorescent lights, her skin looked gray, and her eyes were ringed by dark circles. Feeling apprehensive and trapped, she was on her way to meet a divorce lawyer.

Though on time for her appointment, when she walked into the lawyer's office, she found him taking a bite out of a ham sandwich. With his mouth full, he motioned for her to sit on the opposite side of his massive desk.

She could almost feel his eyes scanning over her as he chewed and swallowed his lunch. He wiped his mouth with the back of his hand and launched into what seemed like a well-rehearsed speech about his expertise as an attorney. She wanted to ask if he'd been through a divorce or if he had children of his own, but the man talked incessantly, making it impossible for her to get a word in. Her eyes drifted to the plaques on the wall, the golf trophies on the shelf, a crayon drawing of a house flanked by two apple trees. The lawyer had lost her attention.

Twenty minutes later, as the man was still rambling on,

Grace shifted uncomfortably in her seat, worrying that a lawyer who charged by the hour was going to be an expensive proposition. As if reading her mind, the attorney stopped mid-sentence and asked if she had a job. When she replied that she was a stay-at-home mother, he emphatically scribbled "unemployed" on his legal pad. Her pulse quickened.

"Motherhood is the hardest job I've ever had; I just don't get paid for it."

The lawyer smiled patronizingly. "You've been out of the workforce for a while, sweetheart, so you'll need to take some vocational training. But don't worry," he smiled again, trying to reassure her, "You're still attractive, so you shouldn't have a problem."

Taking umbrage, she countered, "I am also a fine arts photographer."

"Well," the lawyer replied pointedly, shaking his pen at her, "you can forget about having an artsy-fartsy kind of job. Your obligation now is to be a productive member of society, which means getting a good, steady paycheck. I've got a homework assignment for you," he said. "Find out how much it would cost to hire a nanny to do all the things that you do. You know, cooking, cleaning, driving carpools, homework, all that stuff."

In a daze, Grace walked out of his office, clutching a sheaf of algorithmic charts and settlement strategies. At home, she grew demoralized as she looked through job sites and employment agencies. She wasn't proficient in many computer programs, nor was she an accountant, a grant writer, or a social media whiz. She didn't have barista skills, though she *did* have plenty of experience with childcare. But, at minimum wage, it would cost more to have somebody look after *her* children than she could earn caring for someone else's kids. The lawyer's stern warning rang in her ears: "You've got to get back to the workforce as soon as possible."

Everything she had taken for granted in her life was now up for grabs. *What will I do? What* can *I do?* She put her head down on the table and wept like a bereft child. *I know I'm more than just a paycheck. So much more.*

Driving the school carpool that afternoon, she wore dark glasses, not wanting anyone to see her puffy eyes.

"What snack did you bring today?" the children asked sweetly, knowing that Grace always brought an after-school treat.

"Oatmeal cookies?" suggested the neighbor boy, hopefully.

"Banana muffins?" asked her daughter Rowan, whose two front teeth were missing.

"Maybe it's pineapple day!" shouted little Jimmy, who was only in kindergarten.

"Sorry kids, this was the best I could do today," Grace said, producing a bag of hard pretzels. The children were quiet except for little Jimmy.

"Darn it," he said, obviously disappointed.

In the rearview mirror, Grace saw her daughter give little Jimmy a dirty look. Soon, Grace thought to herself, she wouldn't be able to afford snacks anymore, or even be able to drive the carpool.

A few days later, Grace joined her daughter's class on a school field trip. As a chaperone, her job was to stay at the back of the group, making sure that kids didn't stray.

"Welcome to the Wildlife Rehabilitation Center," chirped their tour guide, "where we care for all types of birds, snakes, and animals like rabbits and foxes. But what most people don't know is that we are also a wolf sanctuary. You'll probably never see one when you come to visit, though, because the wolves live on a huge piece of protected land behind our facility. Believe it or not, they try to avoid humans whenever possible. However," she continued, "you're in luck because we happen to have a gray wolf here in recovery from a gunshot wound."

The guide led the children to a large enclosure. "Please try to keep quiet," she begged of the rambunctious students, who were excited to see the wolf. The animal, lying in the shadowy corner of the cage, was roused by the sound of their voices. She lumbered over to the drinking trough, where she lapped up water with her long, pink tongue.

"Grays are often misunderstood and undervalued by people," the tour guide noted. "Highly intelligent and loyal creatures, they play an important role in the ecosystem.

Unfortunately, they are often killed by humans who are afraid of them." Modulating her voice, the guide stepped away from the cage. "Now, let's go visit a barn owl that's healing from a broken wing."

The children followed the guide, but Grace hung behind, wanting to get a better look at the wolf as she limped back to her resting spot. At close range, Grace could see the animal's wild beauty, and also the sadness in her eyes. Then the wolf raised her head to the sky and let out a howl. The message was perfectly clear: "My body may be injured, but my spirit is free!"

While the children ate lunch at picnic tables outside the visitor's center, Grace realized how good it felt to be distracted from her personal problems.

She noticed a sign for a part-time assistant in the office window, and without missing a beat, applied for the job. A week later, she started working: the pay was good, the atmosphere friendly, her tasks easy. Her favorite part of the job was its proximity to the gray wolf's cage. She and the wolf had a lot in common: they were both in transition, recovering from trauma, and they longed for independence. Over the next few months, she spent as much time as she could around the magnificent creature. Little by little, she could feel a sense of power and purpose growing within her.

One morning, Grace arrived at work to find that the wolf had been released. Though she hadn't been able to say good-bye, it made her happy to think that the animal was roaming free on the land, following her true nature. Picturing the wolf running unfettered through the tall grass, she knew that one day soon, she'd be running free too.

Demeter's Workout

WEARING AN OLD BATHROBE, GRACE STOOD IN THE MIDDLE of her weedy garden on a damp autumn morning, watching a spider spin a web between two branches. Though the natural world was dwindling away, it was the season she loved best. She was deliberately ignoring the cries for attention coming from inside the house: the speckled bananas on the countertop, the empty toilet paper roll, the groaning laundry pile, and the needy little lap dog gnawing on a leather shoe.

The back door opened and her daughter Skye appeared in workout clothes, asking Grace if she wanted to go to the gym. Though she would have been content to idle in the garden, Grace knew not to rebuff this rare invitation from her teenage daughter. She hurried inside to change her clothes before Skye changed her mind.

Brown leaves crunched underfoot as mother and daughter walked together down the sidewalk. Overcome with delight that her daughter wanted to spend time with her, Grace struggled to keep her excitement at bay, knowing all too well the ever-changing moods of an adolescent girl.

As soon as they entered the sleek chrome interior of the gym, Skye moved to the row of treadmills. Gamely, Grace hopped onto the machine next to hers, only to be met with a menacing look that said, "Go away!"

At first, she thought Skye was joking, until she saw the scorching heat coming out of her daughter's eyes. Skye attached her headphones and then disappeared into a hermetically sealed bubble of sound. *Gone.*

Though her pride was wounded, Grace tried to appear unfazed. She sauntered over to the exercise bike, where she fiddled with the seat height, struggling to recover from the sting of rejection. "I never did see the point of a treadmill," she mumbled to herself, "though pedaling a stationary bike doesn't make much sense either."

When she was a girl, her little red bike had been her ticket to freedom and adventure. The clunky machine at the gym, however, was a slog. Up and down imaginary hills she labored, feeling increasingly morose. All around her, people were sweating and straining, grimacing and pushing their way through their exercise routines. She was struck by the pointlessness of it all. *Why even bother trying? Sooner or later, we'll all be dead anyway.*

Her eyes wandered over to Skye's treadmill; it was clear that she wasn't the only one enchanted by her daughter's swinging ponytail and glowing complexion. A cluster of men swarmed in her vicinity, caught in the web of her irresistible maiden energy. Skye, of course, was oblivious to it all.

"It's a bitch, isn't it?" said the woman on the bike next to her. Grace looked askance at the woman who, with her graying hair and thickening waistline, looked a lot like herself.

"It happens every goddamn year," the woman continued, "and still I can't get used to it. Where does the time go, and when did I get so old?"

Nodding in Skye's direction, she added, "Of course, you try to protect them as much as you can, but at some point, you have to let go."

Grace wiped the sweat from her brow but did not reply.

"But that's only half of the story," the woman went on, seeming to read Grace's thoughts. "The real kicker is the grief you feel about losing the part of yourself that was once young and innocent."

From across the room, Skye signaled to her mother that she was ready to leave. Being the faithful old dog that she was, Grace leapt off the bike and joined her.

Out in the open air, they were enticed by the smells coming from the corner bakery. Feeling extravagant, Grace went in and purchased two chocolate croissants. As mother and daughter devoured the buttery treats, they giggled conspiratorially, knowing they were undermining the hard work they'd done at the gym. Through a kaleidoscope of russet, gold, and crimson leaves, they walked back home. Though the natural world was preparing for winter, in Grace's heart it felt like spring.

Pomegranate Season

SUMMER WAS LONG AND RELENTLESS THAT YEAR, AND then, without any notice, everything changed. Autumn rolled into town, sneaking past the drooping sunflowers and sun-bleached grass. Moving stealthily across the landscape, it shook fruits and leaves from the trees and ruffled the feathers of crows, deep in their raucous dreams.

Pulling the cotton blanket over her bare shoulder, Grace shuddered in her sleep. In the morning, after shutting every window in the house with a bang, she rode her bike to the market, listening to the plaintive coo of a mourning dove in a sycamore tree.

Over the past few weeks, she'd guided her shopping cart toward the bins of pears, persimmons, and feijoas, ignoring the sallow pomegranates bearing signs that said, "fresh crop" and "super sweet." As a younger woman, she'd made the mistake of buying pomegranates when they first appeared on the shelves. Being wiser now, she waited for the right moment, when the fruit matured to ripeness.

Emboldened by autumn's arrival, she steered the cart,

wheels wobbling beneath her, directly to the bin of red pomegranates. Instead of taking seeds from the sample tray, she grabbed one of the scarlet orbs and sunk her teeth into its ruby encrusted interior.

The juice tasted bittersweet on her tongue; bright red drops slid down her chin and onto the floor. There was a rumble and a quake, and the ground opened up beneath her feet. Inside the subterranean corridor stood an adolescent girl, her pale hand outstretched toward Grace. With a surprisingly firm grip, the girl maneuvered her through an underground passage filled with stumps and stones, rocks and bones. With each step, Grace was overcome by an inexplicable urge to shed everything she carried—her glasses, earrings, bra, skirt—along with every idea she had about herself.

They squeezed through a narrow cleft in the rock that led to an enormous underground cavern glistening with crystals. The waifish girl dropped Grace's hand and ascended an onyx throne in the middle of the room, where she pulled a shroud-like veil over her face.

Standing naked and vulnerable before the queen, with the darkness pressing in all around her, Grace started to cry. Hot tears of shame and fear splashed onto the cold stone floor. The puddles became pools that turned into an ocean of saltwater. Adrift in waves of sorrow and distress, she began to sink below the surface.

But well before she drowned, the queen snapped her

fingers, and the waters retreated. She pulled Grace onto her lap.

"Am I dying?"

Persephone replied, "You are changing, which is a kind of death."

"I'm scared of change."

"Lift my veil, daughter." the queen commanded.

Slowly and gently, Grace removed the dark fabric that covered the queen's face. Underneath was a dark, empty void.

"You see," the queen said tenderly, "there is 'nothing' to be afraid of."

Placing a cluster of pomegranate seeds in Grace's hand, Persephone said, "Eat these and remember that life is all about change, which allows you to recreate yourself anew, again and again."

Grace stared at the crimson jewels that glittered in the palm of her hand. A strident voice behind her pierced the silence. "Excuse me," it said, with noticeable irritation, "Can you please move over?"

Grace looked up to see that she was back in the market, standing in front of the bin of pomegranates. A middle-aged woman beside her reached out to grab a fistful of seeds from the sample tray. Grace could tell that she, too, was ripe for the descent.

Eternally Yours, Roma

BRUISE-COLORED THUNDERCLOUDS GATHERED OVER VIA Nazionale, where Grace stood waiting for the bus. When the first drops of rain landed hard and fast on her head, she cursed her bad luck. It was the first day of her Roman holiday, and she had forgotten to bring an umbrella.

From the roots of her hair to the soles of her new leather sandals, she was soaked. Her white blouse, now transparent, stuck provocatively to her breasts, which she didn't want to advertise on a crowded Italian bus.

She had hoped to get a seat so she could look out the window as the bus crossed town, but instead she was clinging to a pole, wedged between two sturdy matrons. In the fogged up window, she saw a bedraggled middle-aged woman staring at her. It took a moment for her to realize that she was looking at herself. *What happened to the shiny apple-cheeked girl who used to ride this bus to school every day?*

The bus doors opened at Largo Argentina and the ruins of Pompey's Theater, the locale of Julius Caesar's untimely death on the Ides of March. But Grace also knew that long before that, the area had been a holy shrine devoted to Feronia, the ancient Sabine goddess of fertility. The formerly sacred precinct was now littered with plastic bottles and cigarette butts; it had become a sanctuary for the city's feral cat population.

A nun in full habit sat across the aisle, tapping away on an iPad. Grace looked at her quizzically, wondering what it would be like to be immune to the societal pressure most women faced as they aged.

At the next stop, a wizened old woman got on the bus. With her sharp nose and dark, voluminous clothing, she resembled a huge black crow. Grace averted her gaze.

By the time the bus reached its destination on the Via del Corso, the sun was muscling its way through the clouds. Roman weather, Grace recalled an Italian professor once saying, was as unpredictable as the Old Testament God.

Steam rose from the sidewalk as Grace walked along, lost in thought. She turned down a side street, unable to tell where she was or where she was headed. She passed a small souvenir shop with a sign in the window that read JESUS IS THE WAY. She followed the sound of rushing water that brought her face to face with the sea god Poseidon poised above the roiling waves of the Trevi Fountain. Her stomach lurched. This was where Jack had proposed to her here on a winter night long ago, a moment that changed the trajectory of her life. She was back again, this time on a sweltering day, and the piazza was filled with young people eating gelato and taking selfies. No one noticed her as she passed through the square, headed down a warren of narrow streets. Weary in body and soul, she sat in an outdoor café by the Pantheon, watching the parade of tourists stream by. They fawned over the relics of a bygone civilization, while she examined the ruins of her own life. After drinking a glass of warm Chianti, she signaled the waiter for *il conto*, but was ignored. She tried several times to get his attention until she had a sober realization: *He can't see me because I'm invisible.*

She walked slowly up the Via Veneto to the Capuchin Monastery, where, over many centuries, industrious friars had decorated the underground crypt with the skeletal remains of their deceased brethren, merging the sacred and profane into a bizarre *memento mori*. She wandered through the piles of skulls, astounded at how the monks were able to create beauty out of desolation. *Perhaps grief is the best artist.*

She emerged from the darkness of the catacombs into golden afternoon light. An old woman sat on the church steps, braiding strands of ribbon together. Dressed from head to toe in black, she had a basket on her lap containing three red roses. Grace immediately recognized her as the crone she'd seen on the bus. Reflexively, she reached into her pocket, searching for change. She raised a finger to indicate that she would take *one* of the roses. But the old crone shook her head vigorously, holding up three crooked fingers and cawing insistently, "*Tutto insieme.*" Everything together.

The old woman smiled, and in that moment, her rugged

face beamed with childlike innocence. She thrust the three roses into Grace's arms, rebuffing the money with a wave of her hand. Then the old woman placed the braided circlet on Grace's head. *The crone has given me a crown!*

"*Bella, bella*!" clucked the old woman as she picked up her empty basket and headed toward the bus stop.

Tutto insieme, Grace repeated to herself, looking at the three roses. *Like the phases of my life—maiden, mother, and crone—they all go together.*

Godspeed

AT FIRST GLANCE, DAVID'S HOUSE LOOKED LIKE IT always had. Large terracotta pots filled with rosemary and thyme lined the garden walk, and a laughing Buddha sat on the porch, presiding over an assortment of neatly arranged shoes and boots. Overhead, a lone hawk circled lazily in the blue sky. But as Grace reached the front door of her childhood friend's home, she knew with a sickening certainty that it was no ordinary day.

Not knowing what she would find on the other side of the threshold, Grace knocked apprehensively on the door. She was greeted by an unfamiliar woman who had long, dark hair and deep, soulful eyes. Tibetan bells droned in the background as the woman took Grace's hand and led her down the hallway into the bedroom where David lay unconscious. Surrounded by pills and vials of medicine, it was clear that he was halfway gone and slipping fast.

It was only nine months since David told her about his terminal illness. Standing under blossoming plum trees in her garden, she could not believe the words coming out of his mouth while pink petals swirled around them like confetti.

Grace visited David several times over the summer, though she never stayed long. It was terrifying to watch his bold spirit fade, his strong body taken hostage by the illness. She often brought him treats from his favorite bakery, and when he could no longer eat, she gave him stories to feast on. One day, she told him a hilarious tale that left him choking for air; she knew it did not bode well that humor would have to be taken out of his diet.

David's wife and brother sat huddled together at the foot of the bed, whispering to each other. Grace knelt at the bedside, watching the dark-haired stranger move skillfully around the room, fluffing pillows and wiping sweat from David's brow. All afternoon, the four of them sat around the bed, listening to the dying man's jagged breath. In. Out. In. Out.

From the bedroom window, Grace watched the sun set behind the distant hills. The woman, who had fallen asleep in the rocking chair, woke with a start. She smiled wistfully at Grace before she lifted the covers and got into bed next to David. Holding his frail body in her arms, she kissed him lovingly on the lips. Grace watched with fascination as the woman drew a long, slow breath out of his mouth. His body quivered slightly before becoming perfectly still.

The room filled with a rosy afterglow, and David's wife began to weep. The mysterious woman fled the room, with

Grace not far behind her. She wanted an explanation for what she had just seen, but the woman was nowhere to be found. When Grace asked David's wife and brother where she had gone, they looked confused. Neither of them had noticed her presence, much less her departure.

The holiday season was in full swing, but Grace had no interest in baking, shopping, or parties. Even a trip to the grocery store felt like a major effort. Once, she was caught by surprise in the produce aisle when she heard David's favorite song on the loudspeaker. With a wave of grief rising in her throat, she abandoned her shopping cart and ran outside, barely making it to her car before breaking down in tears. *I can't believe he's gone.*

Throughout the cold days of January, she had little appetite for food or small talk. Her body only craved sleep. In late February, as winter showed its first signs of retreating, she dreamt about David.

I am standing in the doorway of a large room festooned with colorful streamers. People are sitting at long tables laden with bowls of potato chips and trays of sliced watermelon. Someone behind me laughs loudly. I turn around to see David standing there with his goofy grin and riot of curly hair. Overjoyed, I wrap my arms around him. After a moment, I pull back. "I thought you were dead!"

The moment those words tumble out of my mouth, a thick glass wall materializes between us.

"What's it like on the other side?" I ask.

David peers earnestly through the glass and says, "I spend my time saying 'I love you' to everything.

The ringing alarm clock shattered her dream. But for the first time since David's death, she felt relief. *He is all right. I can let him go now.*

The sun poked its way through the branches of the wild plum trees, which of late had bristled with tight magenta buds but were now filled with exquisite pink blossoms.

Looking out into the garden, Grace was startled to see the dark-haired stranger standing under a tree, her pale face raised to the sun, relishing the beauty of that spring morning. Grace did not disturb her in her reverie, knowing that sometime in the future, they would certainly meet again.

Quan Yin Comes to Dinner

DINNERTIME HAD ALWAYS BEEN GRACE'S FAVORITE TIME of day. As a child, she loved sitting elbow-to-elbow, tucked in tight with her parents and five siblings. In addition to the meat and potatoes of physical sustenance, she received a generous helping of belonging and connection around the dining table. There was always a baby in the highchair performing crazy stunts for attention; her brothers had an endless supply of entertaining and inappropriate stories to share. Her father rarely spoke about the place he disappeared to every day—that place called "work," filled with faceless adults, far away from the boisterous clan. And her mother always blessed the meal before launching into her nightly announcements.

These sweet childhood memories came to mind whenever Grace sat down for dinner with her two adolescent daughters. To begin with, it felt awkward sitting around the rectangular table that was much too large for the three of them. Given the hormonal fluctuations of her teenage daughters, Grace never knew what to expect for dinner conversation. Most nights, they ate in silence.

One evening Grace came home from work at a loss to put a meal together. She pulled a familiar box out of the pantry.

"Hey, girls," she said playfully, "how about a little macaroni and cheese tonight?

Skye made a snide comment under her breath.

"This was a special treat when you were little." Grace replied.

"If you haven't noticed, I'm not five years old anymore."

Rowan sat on the couch with her eyes glued to her phone until Grace took it out of her hands.

"Come on, help us get dinner ready."

"Mom, you're *so* annoying!" the girls hissed in unison.

In a knee-jerk reaction, Grace replied, "Whatever."

It was precisely the moment when she could have used some backup. It didn't matter if it was a wise grandmother, a strong man, or even an outspoken friend. All she wanted was another adult to stand by her and say, *Listen to your mother. Show her some respect.*

The light bulb overhead short-circuited with a frizzle and a pop. The metaphor was not lost on her. How was it that a roll of the eyes and a surly comment from her offspring could make her feel so crazy?

She wanted to shout, *What is wrong with you? Somewhere on this planet right now bombs are being dropped, species are going extinct, girls are being forced into slavery. Where's the gratitude?* But she held her tongue.

A trickle of sweat ran down the small of her back. Thanks to perimenopause, she was overheating again. In an act of self-preservation, she moved toward the front door.

The moment she crossed the threshold, her feet lifted effortlessly off the ground. Buoyed by the intoxicating fragrance of night-blooming jasmine, she ascended into the sky, her body dissolving into a flurry of tiny opalescent bubbles. High above the treetops she floated, merging into the purplish light of the gloaming.

Feeling strangely at peace, she asked, "Am I in Heaven?"

"No, my dear, you are simply being held in the thousand-armed embrace of Quan Yin, goddess of compassion."

"But I can't see you . . . where are you?"

"I am everywhere. But seeing me isn't as important as feeling me is."

From her vantage point in the sky, Grace could see skiffs and tankers scattered across the ocean's surface, whales and krakens stirring in the depths below. The mighty mountain ranges behind her were dotted with giant sequoias and redwoods. Directly below her, traffic flowed like a red river of light.

"What do you see down there?" Quan Yin asked gently.

"Ugh, too many cars on the highway."

"Look deeper," the goddess of compassion encouraged. "What if I told you that each of those cars is filled with someone on a mission of love: coming home from a job that feeds their family, picking up their kids from school, visiting a friend in the hospital? What if you were able to see that everyone is driving toward some greater goal for themselves and the ones they love? Look around you," Quan Yin suggested. "What do you see?"

Suddenly, Grace was standing in the kitchen with her two daughters, aware of pulsating lights emanating from each of their hearts. These tiny, laser-like beams moved back and forth between their bodies, creating complex geometric patterns in the space between them. In a moment of clarity, she understood that beneath the layered clothing, headphones, and posturing, there existed a love far greater than she could comprehend. Despite the disguises they wore and the roles they played, a profound and powerful force wove her little family together.

Like an improvisational actor, Grace knew how to change the dynamic. "Let's hit the reset button."

Her daughters looked up, startled.

"OK, girls, what should we do about dinner?"

Skye wanted pancakes. Rowan wanted to eat dinner sitting by the fireplace.

The girls set to work with an uncharacteristic vigor, collecting wood, arranging pillows, stirring batter.

After licking the syrup off her fingers, Grace pulled out a stack of old photo albums. Together they laughed and cooed at images of their younger selves. The girls pored over Grace's high school yearbook, teasing her about her clothes and hairstyle. They were eager to know about her first boyfriend, the arguments she'd had with her parents, the silly things she'd done with her friends. They seemed surprised to find that she, too, had once been a teenager.

Since it was a school night, the girls untangled themselves reluctantly off the couch and retreated upstairs to bed. Grace sat in a quiet living room, basking in the glow of the fire. Who knew that tonight's dinner would go down as one of the best meals of all time?

Un Coeur Ouvert
(An Open Heart)

RUBBERY CARROTS.

Leaky Chinese food container.

Empty pickle jar.

It was a Sunday morning in May, and Grace was cleaning out the refrigerator. Though it felt good to clear things out, she also felt a nagging guilt that she assumed was a vestige from her Catholic upbringing. Though she had gone to church every Sunday morning of her childhood, the idea of going voluntarily as an adult had never interested her.

Through the partially opened back door, a sliver of lemony light wedged itself onto the kitchen floor. Al Green's soulful voice wafted through the air. *I'm so tired of being alone.*

She knew she had so much to be grateful for: a healthy family, food on the table, and a sunny little cottage to call home. But she couldn't shake the feeling that there was something missing. She was living in "the safe zone," floating along a backwater tributary instead of shooting the rapids of life. By avoiding risk, she hoped to protect herself from heartbreak and loss.

"I guess that's how it goes when you've got kids to raise," she said out loud to an empty room. The word *ennui* popped into her head. *The French have a word for everything.* She thought about Caroline, her best friend who lived in Paris. Impulsively, she picked up the phone.

"*Bonsoir*?"

"Hey, sweetie. I was just thinking about you and wanted to say hi."

"Oh, Gracie!" Caroline exclaimed breathlessly, "So good to hear your voice! Martin and I have been out at the jazz festival all day. The Left Bank is simply bursting with music. The weather is perfect, not too hot yet."

"Spring in Paris sounds wonderful."

"What about you, *ma chérie*? How are your darling children? Do you have anything fun planned for summer?"

"Well, first of all," Grace answered with a laugh, "I rarely put the words 'darling' and 'teenager' together in the same sentence! Anyway, we're all fine. The girls are going away with their dad for two weeks in June, and I'm looking forward to having some time to myself. You know, to clean out my sock drawer, do yoga, eat popcorn for dinner . . . that sort of thing."

"*Non, non, non*." (Her friend sounded very French when she said that.) "That won't do! You simply must come to Paris while your daughters are away!"

"Well," Grace replied dubiously, "That *would* be nice, wouldn't it?"

When she hung up, Grace paced from the kitchen to the living room and back again, deep in contemplation. *Could I?* She opened the backdoor and sat on the steps in a patch of sunlight. She had the time, she had some money stashed away, so what else was there to hold her back?

Many years ago, when Grace was pregnant with Skye, Caroline had married a Frenchman and moved to Paris. Caught in the endless cycle of diaper changes, Grace often fantasized about her friend's charmed life across the sea. She imagined her riding a vintage bike through the Latin Quarter, a fresh baguette and a bouquet of daisies peeking out of her tote bag. With a good job, a husband who adored her, an assortment of fascinating friends, and a weekend home in the Breton countryside, Caroline had a good life all in all. A trip to Paris had never seemed feasible to Grace, until now.

Exactly a month later, Grace found herself on an Air France flight bound for Charles de Gaulle, listening to French language lessons on her headphones. She was making furious notes in the margins of her Paris guidebook: *Paris Plages, Pompidou Center, Fondation Louis Vuitton, Bois De Boulogne, Sainte-Chapelle, the Louvre, Mariage Frères.*

Her excitement grew as the taxi threaded its way through the city. When the driver stopped in front of an elegant building with a mansard roof, she almost pinched herself. *Ten days in Paris—here I come!*

Caroline squealed in delight when Grace arrived. "I have to warn you," she said, "Martin has his friends over, and they're watching Wimbledon." The way she rolled her eyes revealed that she couldn't care less about sports.

A cluster of men sat in the living room; their eyes were glued to the television. When the two women entered, the men all stood up. Grace noticed that each one wore a pair of pressed jeans, a button-down shirt, and freshly polished loafers. Feeling unkempt after the long flight, she excused herself to the bathroom, where she splashed cold water on her face.

Caroline showed her to a tiny, sparsely furnished room. "We call this the hermit's cell. The main thing is that the bed is comfortable. There's a nice view of the Luxembourg Gardens from the balcony. But trust me, you're not going to be spending much time in here! By the way, are you seeing anyone?"

"No, after my divorce, I don't think I can bear any more heartache."

Martin popped his head in the doorway. "The tennis match is over and we're going out for pizza. You lovely ladies are welcome to join us, though I understand if you prefer to stay here and catch up."

"*Allons-y,*" Grace replied enthusiastically, happy to show off one of the few phrases she knew in French.

Martin clapped his hands together. "*C'est bon!*"

The women walked arm in arm through the Left Bank, chattering like parakeets. The streets teemed with people enjoying the warm summer evening. Catching a scent of sautéed garlic and butter, Grace realized that she hadn't eaten anything since leaving California.

At the restaurant, she sat between Caroline and Jean-Claude, one of Martin's oldest friends. After a few sips of red wine, she could feel the jet lag catching up with her. Jean-Claude asked her a question in French, but seeing the blank expression on her face, repeated it in English. "Is this conversation boring you?"

"No! I'm just very tired." Grace explained. "I can barely think in English right now, let alone French!"

Jean-Claude patted her hand. "I completely understand."

She flushed, miraculously getting a second wind. "You speak English very well."

"I have lived my whole life in Paris, though I go to England quite often for work. I've also been to America several times, but only the East Coast. I would love to visit California one day, the land of surfing and movie stars." Jean-Claude continued, "Tell me, do you know Paris well?"

"Not really." she replied. "I haven't been here since college. We were pretty low budget back then. We had to walk to the top of the Eiffel Tower because we couldn't afford to take the elevator."

Jean-Claude laughed. "How about I show you around while you're here? Then you can return the favor when I come to California."

The next morning, Grace paced back and forth in front of Saint-Sulpice waiting for Jean-Claude to arrive, feeling an uncomfortable dampness under her arms. *Is this a hot flash or am I nervous?* Jean-Claude waved enthusiastically from down the block. "Let's start our grand tour with a little caffeine, shall we?" he called out.

They walked to a nearby café, where Jean-Claude ordered two coffees. With his elbow resting on the marble countertop, he asked, "So, what is your pleasure? Renoir or Rimbaud? Do you prefer Marie Antoinette or Madame Curie? Are you interested in *parfum*? *Opéra*? Couture? Eco-architecture?"

She was dumbstruck; she was used to being asked what was for dinner, or who was driving the carpool, or if there were any clean socks . . . but it was rare for anyone to ask her about her interests. Out of her purse she pulled the bucket list she had compiled on the airplane.

"Très formidable," Jean-Claude said playfully as he read over the list. It will take us at least a month to get through it." He winked. "We'd better get started."

As they crossed the Pont des Arts, Grace pointed to parapets bristling with thousands of small padlocks. "Is this some kind of art installation?"

"*Non*, these are called 'love locks.' The idea is that lovers profess their devotion to each other by attaching a lock to the bridge and throwing the key into the river."

'Oh, that's sweet," she replied.

Jean-Claude paused briefly before he responded. "Actually," he said, "I do not approve. You see, the weight of the locks compromises the integrity of the bridge." With a hint of scorn in his voice, he said, "These people don't understand what love is. To love is to want the other to be free. You cannot lock away love and throw away the key!"

He turned to her and asked, "Are you married?"

"No," she answered. "You?"

"*Non.*"

An awkward silence hung between them, broken only when Jean-Claude pointed out the Louvre. Grace smiled, she couldn't help but notice that Jean-Claude was a natural guide: funny, animated, and passionate.

"Are you religious?" he asked.

"I was raised Catholic, but I don't go to church much anymore." *What is he getting at?*

"Would you mind if I showed you my mother's favorite church in all of Paris? Église de la Madeleine; it's just ahead."

With its commanding portico of columns and sculpted pediment, the building looked more like a Greek temple than a Catholic church. When they entered the darkened interior, they were greeted by a deep, resonant blast of the pipe organ. "We're in luck," Jean-Claude whispered. He took her arm and led her to the front pew, where they sat listening to the music. Jean-Claude got up, genuflected in front of the altar, and went to light a candle at the small shrine. Disarmed by this touching gesture, Grace closed her eyes in prayer until Jean-Claude returned to her side, letting her know that he was ready to leave.

They stepped into blinding sunlight outside of the church.

"Come," Jean-Claude said playfully. "I want to show you something."

He led her to an unmarked green door on the outside of the church and put his finger to his lips. "This is a hidden café that not many tourists know about. It is completely run by volunteers. Would you like to see it?"

At a small table under a vaulted ceiling, Jean-Claude said, "When I was a child, my mother would bring me here every Saturday morning to pray to the Magdalene. Afterwards we always came to the café for lunch."

"Does she still…?"

Jean-Claude replied abruptly, "My mother passed away when I was at university."

"And your father?"

"He died when I was a little boy."

"I'm so sorry," Grace offered feebly.

"Ah well, it was a long time ago." He shrugged. "Perhaps this is why I have never left Paris. All of my memories are here." Jean-Claude looked down at his hands, intently inspecting his fingernails. Grace wanted to put her arms around him, but the space was cramped, and besides, she barely knew him.

The waiter brought out two small ramekins of chocolate mousse to the table. Dipping her spoon into the dessert, Grace admitted, "When I went to Catholic school as a child, we were taught that Mary Magdalene was a prostitute. I'm afraid I really don't know much about her at all."

Jean-Claude looked at her with sad eyes, as if this admission hurt him personally. "That is such a pity. You see, in France, we have a strong tradition of Magdalene devotion, particularly in Provence, where my mother was born. Mary Magdalene is said to have lived there after Jesus died. To this day she is still revered as a powerful teacher and healer."

"Really? I never knew that."

"I remember my mother taking me to Magdalene pilgrimage sites—Montségur and Saintes-Marie-de-la-Mer. One time, she even took me to Saint-Maximin-la-Sainte-Baume on Magdalene's feast day, thinking I would enjoy the candlelight procession of Magdalene's skull through the town. But seeing the skull they claim was hers gave me horrible nightmares. It was unthinkable to me that this holy woman had been carved up into pieces after she died."

Shaking his head, he continued, "I do not understand the penchant for relics. Did you know that they have one of her teeth at the Metropolitan Museum of Art? I saw it for myself the last time I was in New York."

Deeply engrossed in the conversation, Grace didn't notice that the waiters were cleaning tables and closing up the cafe. *Where had the time gone?*

"Can we continue our tour another day?" Jean-Claude asked. "There are still more things I'd like to show you."

"Of course!" she replied, her face flushing with heat.

The following Sunday morning, Jean-Claude sat outside of Caroline's apartment. waiting for Grace to emerge. She hopped on the back of his scooter, wrapping her arms tightly around him as they wove their way through the Left Bank toward Notre Dame cathedral.

Except for churchgoers and eager tourists, the streets were empty.

"Do you know that many people, my mother included, believe Notre Dame was originally a shrine to Mary Magdalene?" Jean-Claude said.

"I had no idea," Grace replied. "You could give Magdalene tours!" she added teasingly. "You know so much about the subject."

Jean-Claude ushered her into the cathedral. After admiring the rose window, he led her to a small side chapel to see a painting of Mary Magdalene washing the feet of Jesus. Once again, he lit a votive candle and knelt in prayer. "Let's take a walk to the Louvre," he suggested. "I want to introduce you to a dear friend of mine."

Inside the museum, Jean-Claude led her into a gallery of Renaissance art. Instinctively, she moved toward a life-sized statue hidden in an alcove. She was vaguely aware of Jean-Claude saying, "Good, you've found her! I will leave you two to get acquainted."

Grace slowly approached the polychromed image of a woman covered by a mane of long golden hair. The placard at her feet read, "Sainte Marie Madeleine: ascétique mystique, 1515 A.D." Though she admired the Magdalene's graceful posture and subtly painted skin tones, she did not fully appreciate the sculpture until she looked into its eyes. Feeling a rush of energy surge through her body, Grace put her hands on her heart. In her mind's eye, she could see all the padlocks on Pont des Arts springing open. *Magdalene is opening my heart, freeing me to love again.* She stood there for several minutes, tears of gratitude falling from her eyes. And then she was aware of Jean-Claude standing by her side.

"Something has come up at work," he said, his cell phone in his hand, "and I must go immediately. I'm so sorry!" He kissed her on both cheeks and was gone.

GRACE FLOATED ON a cloud all the way back to the Left Bank, looking with fresh eyes at everything around her: the lovers entwined on a park bench, the taxi driver having a cigarette break, the accordion player counting the coins in his open valise.

Back at the apartment, while Grace raved about her sightseeing tour with Jean-Claude, Caroline had a slight frown on her face as she concentrated on pouring two glasses of Burgundy.

"That man is a treasure."

"He really is," agreed Caroline, handing Grace a glass of wine.

"Tell me more about him."

The hint of a shadow flitted across Caroline's face. "Well, what can I say? Jean-Claude is like a brother to Martin. We love him very much."

Before Grace could ask another question, Caroline raised her glass for a toast.

"Here's to *our* friendship, which has stood the test of time. I'm so glad you decided to come to Paris. If you had stayed home, you would have missed out big time!"

"So true! I've loved every minute!"

"To love," Caroline proclaimed. "As they say in France, *l'amour est plus fort que la mort,* love is stronger than death."

All too soon, Grace's big adventure was coming to an end. She couldn't deny feeling sad that she hadn't spent more time with Jean-Claude, who was out of town on business.

On her last night in Paris, Grace tagged along to a party in the Marais. Because it was stifling hot inside the apartment, Grace and Caroline sat out on the tiny balcony. A warm hand alighted on Grace's bare shoulder. *Jean-Claude.*

"Did you think I would let you leave Paris without saying good-bye?"

Caroline excused herself to find Martin, and Jean-Claude sat down next to Grace.

"My dear," he said, taking her hand. "I have a question. How would you like to come back to France for Christmas?"

"Oh, that's so sweet of you, but . . ." she demurred. "I can't. I have my kids."

"Or maybe you could come back next summer? We

could take a trip to Provence. We could go on a Magdalene pilgrimage together. It would be so much fun. You see," he said, lowering his voice, "I feel that we are *sympathique,* and I want to know you better." He leaned over and kissed her lightly on the lips.

Her mind went blank. *Did he just kiss me?*

Then her mind started to spin out of control. *Maybe when the kids are in college, I'll move to France, and we will live happily ever after. . . .*

Common sense returned. *Get real, he doesn't even know my last name.*

"I care for you, too," she stammered, searching for a diplomatic response. "Let me think about it."

After trading phone numbers and addresses, Caroline took Grace by the arm. "Come on, girl! Let's get you home to bed before your taxi arrives at the crack of dawn."

By sunrise, Grace was boarding her flight home, excited to see her daughters again. But her mind kept returning to thoughts of Jean-Claude.

Once back in California, her life resumed with alarming regularity, though she was determined not to let the memories of her Parisian adventure fade away. She smoothed a piece of red velvet over the top of her dresser and created a small altar. On top of it, she placed a bouquet of red roses in a vase that had once belonged to her grandmother. Every morning and every evening, she lit a candle and said a prayer to the Magdalene.

Caroline called the next week to say that she missed Grace. "I think someone else is missing you too."

Ah yes, Jean-Claude.

"The two of you really hit things off."

"Yes," Grace agreed, her voice giddy. "Right before I left, he invited me to visit him in Provence next summer."

There was a pause on the other end of the line.

"So, he didn't tell you?"

"Tell me what?"

"Listen, I don't know how to say this, but Jean-Claude has an inoperable brain tumor. He's known about it for a year; the doctors say that there's nothing they can do."

Grace slumped into the couch. *That would explain his intensity. The man is a ticking time bomb.*

"Don't tell him that I told you," Caroline demanded.

A few days later, Grace found a hand-written letter from Jean-Claude in her mailbox. Though it was filled with news about his life in Paris, it said nothing about his health. She immediately wrote back, telling him about her kids, her dog, her Magdalene shrine. The correspondence whizzed back and forth across the Atlantic, weaving their two worlds together. Every night, she repeated her mantra when she lit the votive candle: *My heart is open, my heart is open, my heart is open.*

Jean-Claude sent her lavender soap from Provence, she sent him a Hollywood star map. She mentioned that she'd lit a candle for him at the shrine of St. Jude, the patron saint of lost causes. But never once did he allude to his illness.

IT WAS A frosty morning early in the new year when Grace's phone rang. Assuming that it was Jean-Claude on the line, she breathed into the receiver, "*Bonjour, mon amour.*"

"Uh, hi, it's me, Caroline." Her voice was hoarse.

"Oh, hi!" Grace replied casually, though her face was red with embarrassment. "What's up?"

"Umm. I thought you'd want to know that Jean-Claude had a stroke in the night and died. Martin and I are absolutely gutted."

"*What*? That can't be."

"I'm so sad I can't talk right now," Caroline sputtered, ending the call.

Grace stood in the living room, clutching her phone to her chest, as if it could stop her heart from breaking. Not knowing what to do, she walked upstairs to her bedroom. She methodically pulled a box of matches out of the drawer and lit the beeswax candle on her altar. She picked up the postcard Jean-Claude had recently sent. On the front was a picture of the love locks on the Pont des Arts. On the back of the card was written a quote from Albert Camus: "*C'est cela l'amour, tout donner tout sacrifier sans espoir de retour.*" She brushed the tears out of her eyes, realizing the truth of these words: But that's love, to give everything, to sacrifice everything without the slightest desire to get anything in return.

Mighty Aphrodite

GRACE HURRIED OUT THE FRONT DOOR TO THE CAR, WHERE Skye sat in the front seat, staring intently at her phone.

Skye scowled. "What the hell, Mom! Have you completely lost your senses?"

"Huh?"

"If we're late to my appointment because of you, I swear I'll never forgive you."

"Well, that's a little extreme, don't you think?" Grace said.

"I can't depend on you for anything."

"But, honey, we've got plenty of time. You'll be there early, I promise." Gripping the leather steering wheel, Grace stared steely-eyed out the windshield. *What the hell is wrong with my daughter?*

Skye had spent most of the morning sequestered in the bathroom, doing the preliminary primping and preening for the prom. Between the nail polishing, the face mask, and the hair treatment, she had been too busy to walk the dog or help with the breakfast dishes.

"Are you feeling all right?" Grace asked. "You know you can talk to me about anything."

"*No!*" Skye shrieked.

The silence that followed felt heavy, even a little bit dangerous.

"So then, what's the plan for tonight?" Grace asked tentatively. "Is your date picking you up? Do you need to get him a boutonniere?"

Skye rounded on her furiously, "I told you I don't know the plan yet, so stop asking me!"

Grace pulled up in front of the hair salon, her voice strained. "Here we are, seven minutes early. I told you not to worry."

"Pick me up in an hour," her daughter commanded, slamming the car door behind her. Grace clamped her lips together, afraid of what might slip out of her mouth.

Without pausing, she drove over to the plant nursery, where she had a tradition of buying herself a rosebush for Mother's Day every year. Although fragrance and color had always been important considerations when choosing a rose, this year Grace picked one solely for its name, Mighty Aphrodite. She carried her new purchase carefully back to the car. As she placed it in the backseat, she pricked her finger on a thorn. On the verge of tears, she stuck her bloody finger into her mouth. *I'm so hormonal! She's so hormonal! But damn it, I won't let anyone treat me like that!*

Mad now as well as sad, she sat in the parked car, thinking about how her daughter would go off to college in a few short months. *I don't want it to end like this.*

Skye was waiting in the parking lot, looking angelic with her hair falling in lustrous curls around her face. She hopped into the passenger seat, and before Grace could speak her mind, Skye apologized.

"Sorry, Mom, for getting mad at you earlier," she said. "I'm just feeling a lot of stress right now."

Caught off guard, Grace replied, "It's OK, sweetie." *How easily a mother forgives.*

"Here's the plan," said Skye. "We're going to the park at six for photos, and then we're going to take a car service to the prom. That way no one has to drive."

"That sounds good. Remind me of your date's name again?"

"Max."

"Where's Max going to college?"

"Uh, I don't know."

You don't know?

One of the many things that confounded Grace about high school was that, unlike elementary school, she barely knew any of her children's friends. *Just who is this young man, Max? A stoner? A player? A troublemaker?* She decided it was best not to ask too many questions.

She deposited the rosebush on the front porch, pleased to find that some of the green sepals on the buds had already started to curl back, revealing a blush of color beneath. *With a little more time and sunshine, the roses will bloom.* Then she noticed a single rose peeking out from behind a mass of glossy leaves. "Wow," she said out loud, "Mighty Aphrodite indeed!" She bent over, sticking her nose deep into its calyx.

Lost in olfactory bliss, she was startled by a voice.

"Take time for pleasure!" it said.

Grace lifted her head from the flower.

Who said that?

Eager for another helping of its exquisite fragrance, she bent over the flower. Once again, she heard the voice, which seemed to be coming from inside the rose.

"Pleasure is a gateway that leads you back to yourself. But you have to cultivate it!"

"Hmmm," she mused. "Sensuality hasn't been high on my list, but I could change that!"

"And remember," the tiny voice giggled, "never let the thorns stop you from blooming."

Grace went inside and put on her favorite dress. The soft, forgiving fabric always made her feel good when she wore it. For good measure, she brushed her hair and put a dash of French perfume behind her ears.

Skye walked into the room. "Wow, Mom, you look nice! Are you going somewhere?"

"Not really," Grace replied nonchalantly.

"Can I have some of that?" Skye asked, reaching for the perfume bottle. "It smells really good!"

At the park, glamorous young women in sparkly gowns

paraded across the lawn, their heels sinking into the grass. Young men, uncomfortable in their tuxedos, gathered at the periphery, looking terrified of their gorgeous dates.

Skye tottered out of the car in a vintage dress that accentuated her hourglass figure. She waved at a gangly boy in a red bow tie standing next to a woman wearing an oversized sweater.

"Hi, I'm Max's mom!" the woman said. "Has anyone ever told you that you and your daughter look exactly alike?"

Skye turned away, pretending not to hear.

Max's mom pulled a phone out of her purse. "Smile, I want to take some prom pictures."

"C'mon, Mom," Max complained. "Don't take forever."

"My mom does the same thing," Skye agreed. "It's so embarrassing."

Looking at Max's mom, Grace joked, "We have so much to learn from our children, don't we?"

After the photos were taken, Grace walked back to her car, admiring bright Venus in the darkening sky. Her stomach rumbled, reminding her that she had forgotten to eat lunch. Thinking of the advice she had gotten from the rose, she decided to treat herself to a nice dinner. With her head held high, she walked into a fancy Italian restaurant and asked for a table for one.

"Of course, madame," said the solicitous waiter, showing her to a cozy candlelit table by the wall.

"Can I interest you in a drink?"

"Yes, I'll have a glass of red wine."

"I have just the thing for you," said the waiter, smiling. "Something luscious and full-bodied."

"I like the sound of that." she replied.

The waiter returned to the table carrying a wine glass filled with deep red liquid. With a dramatic flourish, he announced, "A glass of Venus de Milo for a very beautiful lady." Grace smiled, knowing that Venus was another name for Aphrodite. Though everything on the menu looked delicious, she decided on the artichoke hearts and fettuccine with prawns. She ate her meal with gusto, mopping up the leftover garlic sauce with a hunk of bread.

As was his nightly custom, the chef came out of the kitchen to greet the restaurant patrons. When he stopped at Grace's table, she told him in faltering Italian that she had once lived in Italy. "*Non parlo molto bene, ma abitavo a Roma venticinque anni fa.*" Impressed by her language skills, the chef arranged for a sumptuous goblet of tiramisu to be brought to her table. The waiter winked at her, saying, "It's on the house."

When she left the restaurant, the chef kissed her hand and murmured "*Que bella donna.*" Satiated by the good meal and the attention that she received at dinner, Grace was feeling euphoric when she pulled up to the house. As she passed the rosebush on the front porch, she whispered to it, "Mighty Aphrodite, I can already tell that you're having a good influence on me."

Taking Off the Wetsuit

GRACE AND HER FRIEND EMILY HAD A TRADITION OF GOING out for coffee on the day after Christmas. For Emily, it was an excuse to take a break from her in-laws, but for Grace it was an acknowledgement that she had made it through yet another holiday as a single mom. This year, as the women sat huddled together at a marble-topped table, talking about books and movies, a handsome stranger approached. Emily introduced Joe as one of her colleagues from work. Joe shook Grace's hand firmly, saying that he liked her scarf. Grace returned the compliment, saying that she liked his cap.

"It was a Christmas gift," Joe replied.

"Mine too!" Grace exclaimed, smiling broadly.

When Joe excused himself from the table, Grace unbuttoned her sweater.

"Well, look who's flushing!" Emily said with a sly grin, "Or are you flashing? It's hard to tell these days."

"Neither!" Grace shot back. "It's just hot in here."

On the afternoon of New Year's Eve, she ran into Joe at

the grocery store, which was packed with people buying food and alcohol for parties. "You're wearing my favorite red scarf!" he called out from across the aisle.

A few days later, she saw him again at the bank, and waved from across the room.

EMILY CALLED HER that night. "Joe tells me that you two keep bumping into each other."

"Yeah, it's kind of funny."

"He's a sweetie pie. *And* he's single, you know."

Grace's heart fluttered. "Oh really?" Trying to sound nonchalant, she asked, "Did he recently move into the neighborhood?"

"He's lived around here as long as I've known him. Maybe it's just the universe trying to get your attention," Emily teased.

"Maybe," Grace repeated, remembering the wish she had recently made for a companion and lover. *Maybe that's why I keep running into him?*

She returned regularly to the coffeehouse where she first met Joe, hoping that she might bump into him there again. Before long, it seemed that the universe was indeed conspiring to grant her wish. They sat at the community table sipping their lattes and getting to know each other. Grace studied the shape of his face. She liked his energy, his easy laugh. When he spoke about surfing as a spiritual experience, she noticed how his eyes lit up. Something twanged in her lower belly—was it *mittelschmerz,* the sensation she felt when she ovulated? Or perhaps it was the stirring of her atrophied muscle of desire?

They met for drinks a few times before Joe invited her over for dinner. With a glass of chardonnay in hand, she browsed through his record collection while he put the finishing touches on dinner. Just before they were about to eat, Joe touched the scarf around her neck and said, "Let me help you take off your armor." With that simple gesture, all her defenses melted.

After that, days and weeks moved into hyperdrive as Grace's system flooded with rogue endorphin rushes, which was at once glorious and agonizing. When alone in her car, she listened to corny love songs on the radio. *I should not be operating heavy machinery.* She painted her toenails red; she splurged on a pair of flirty wedges. Her new health regime included early morning jogs, face masks, and spirulina smoothies.

Winter turned to spring, and like the flamboyant blossoming of the magnolia trees, the affair flowered. The world suddenly felt hopeful and fresh. Grace was falling under Cupid's seductive spell. *Could this be love?*

Yet despite the intensity of those good feelings, her happiness was shadowed by self-doubt. She found herself holding back from Joe, mostly because she was terrified of making the same mistakes she had in her marriage.

One warm May evening, as they sat in an outdoor cafe, Joe reached across the table and took her hand.

"Oh," he said with eyes shining, "I'm so crazy about you."

Before she could respond, the waiter materialized, asking if they wanted another round of drinks. (Yes, they did, thank you.) Not knowing what to say, she changed the subject, returning to the story she had been telling before being interrupted.

Later that evening, she called her friend Emily in distress.

"Hey, lovebird," Emily said. "How are you doing?"

Grace answered feebly, "I'm all right."

"What's up? Everything's OK with Joe?"

"He's fine . . . it's just that I don't know where this is going. And honestly, I'm not sure I ever want to get married again."

"Whoa! Wait a minute! Don't get ahead of yourself," Emily said. "This is your first relationship after your divorce. You've got to take it slow. Enjoy the moment, you know, go with the flow."

"Bingo," Grace thought to herself. *But how do I do that?*

The next day, she went cruising down the self-help aisle at a local bookstore. She accidentally knocked over a book called *Prayers to the Orishas* which, after falling to the ground with a loud *thunk,* opened to a page bearing the image of a dark-skinned goddess walking across the moonlit sea. Below the picture was a prayer:

Yemanja, queen of the seas, mother of all,
Let your sacred waters wash over me.
Cleanse me, nurture me, sustain me,
Yemanja, mistress of the moon.
Shine your healing light on my doubts and fears,
So that I may truly love again.

This was exactly the wisdom Grace had been looking for! She tucked the book under her arm, committed to learning the prayer by heart.

That night, she sat alone in the backyard looking up at the moon, thinking about Jean-Claude and Joe, and the fact that she knew so little about love.

Joe called early the next morning. "Let's take a trip out to the beach! It's going to be a scorcher today."

They drove to the coast, windows wide open, singing along with the radio. Once at the beach, Joe became visibly excited.

"Last one in is a rotten egg!" he shouted, peeling off his clothes and sprinting to the water as if to embrace a long-lost lover. He bounded through the sun-splashed waves, whooping and hollering with joy. Grace dipped her toes in at the water's edge and shivered. She envied the way Joe plunged into the ocean, a metaphor for how he lived his life.

"What have you got to lose?" he shouted over the waves to her.

Good question.

Gathering her courage, she stepped into the water, chanting to herself.

"Let your sacred waters wash over me."

She was up to her waist when a large wave came barreling toward her. As it approached, she saw that the wave was made up of thousands of lacy ruffles—*just like Yemanja's dress!* The goddess was perched on top of the wave, radiant as the sun.

"Do not be afraid!" she called out to Grace. "I have come to bring you back into the flow. Surrender to my healing waters."

Lifting the hem of her flounced dress, the goddess urged her to dive in. Energized by the cold water, Grace became buoyant and playful like a dolphin; she swam quickly out to meet her lover.

"I thought you were never coming in. You're as slow as molasses!"

"Better late than never," Grace answered, splashing Joe with an arc of water.

A large wave crested above them, and together they bodysurfed to the shore, where they collapsed in laughter on the sand. In high spirits, Grace called out, "Thank you, Yemanja!" before she picked herself up from the churning foam, ready to catch the next wave.

Out on a Limb

THE GOLDEN SUN ROSE TRIUMPHANTLY OVER THE HILLS, illuminating rooftops that glittered with frost. From where she stood, just over the kitchen sink, Grace called out to Rowan to come have a look.

Rowan groaned in exasperation. "How can it be March and still so cold?" she complained. "It's been *such* a long winter."

"Long winter, California style," Grace added. "But don't worry, spring will come. It always does."

She was about to remind Rowan not to leave the house with wet hair when the carpool showed up, and her daughter rushed out the front door. Carrying the dirty breakfast dishes to the sink, Grace wondered why she still bothered trying to give motherly advice. After all, Rowan was almost seventeen years old and fully capable of making her own decisions. One more year of high school, and then she'd be gone. Grace shook her head, unable to fathom the prospect of an empty nest.

The dog pawed at her leg. *It's my turn now.*

With her breath billowing like smoke in the cold morning air, Grace walked the dog around the block. Though tufts of oxalis, reliable harbingers of Spring, sprouted up on the side of the road, their blossoms remained firmly closed. Bare trees raised a latticework of dark branches against the pale blue sky.

"Soon, they will all return: the wisteria, the irises, the sweet peas. Soon," she repeated out loud, in a voice tinged with melancholy. "I hope it comes soon."

She prayed quietly, as she often did, when she took the dog out for a walk. That morning it helped soften the discouragement she felt when she thought of all the little deaths that made up her life. When she thought of Joe, she found herself missing him. Last year they had been in the middle of a wonderful affair, but then he accepted his dream job in Atlanta and moved away. Though he was keen to continue the relationship, Grace did not want long-distance love, nor was she willing to uproot her family to be with him. Wistfully she had let go of Joe, though she wondered what might have happened if he had stayed.

She returned home to find a man in a green jumpsuit standing in front of her house.

"You live here?" he inquired. "I'm here to let you know that my guys are coming tomorrow to take this tree down." he said, pointing at the large Monterey pine that stood on the green strip in front of her house.

"Why? What's wrong with it?" she said, her voice rising in alarm. "The tree seems perfectly fine to me!"

"Look, lady," the man shrugged, "I'm just doing my job. You can call my boss if you have any questions."

The supervisor on the other end of the phone line was unfazed by Grace's interrogation.

"With this type of tree," the woman drawled, "especially when it's as old as this one is, it most likely has a beetle or fungal infestation. Our protocol is to take these trees down before they come crashing down." Before Grace could try to plead with her, the woman added, "The tree is on city property, so there's nothing you can do about it anyway."

Feeling like she'd been punched in the stomach, Grace leaned against the tree's craggy trunk, looking up at the strong branches that formed a green canopy over the house, protecting it from the summer heat and sheltering it from the busy road. The tree was her friend: it was the last thing she saw when she left the house each day and the first thing to greet her when she came home.

BY NIGHTFALL, ONE thing was certain; it was time to say good-bye. Barefoot, Grace walked outside and wrapped her arms around the doomed tree, which stood tall and luminous in the moonlight. As she whispered her gratitude, she heard a rustling noise in the treetop. A shadowy figure moved from branch to branch until it rested on a bough directly above her head. She looked up inquiringly at the little man whose hair was adorned with foliage.

"You don't need to worry." he said in a stage whisper, his voice at once tender and husky.

"I'm not," she replied, noticing the greenish hue of his skin. "But this beautiful tree is going to be cut down in a few hours!"

"Yes, I know," he said with a laugh. "Its time has come. Haven't you seen the death caps and the destroying angel mushrooms around the base of the tree? They've been midwifing this old girl for a while." He patted the trunk with admiration. "She's ready to go, too. Already sent her vital energy into the root network to nourish the other trees in the area," he said proudly. "Don't be sad," he said with a childlike sweetness, "because if things didn't die, there wouldn't be room for anything new to be born."

The next morning, Grace was awakened by a chorus of chainsaws roaring into action. She and Rowan dressed, had breakfast, and left the house as quickly as possible. Though she tried to avert her gaze, she could not help but notice the fallen branches, looking like severed limbs, on the side of the road.

She did not return home until it was growing dark. Though there was a lingering scent of pine in the air, every needle and flake of sawdust had been swept up. Nothing was left of her mighty tree other than the pitiful stump at her feet. She reached out to touch its heartwood, feeling that her own heart was about to break. Over her head was a yawning expanse of nothingness. But as her eyes adjusted to the darkness, she noticed a star, and another, and another until she realized that the vast sky was filled with stars she was never been able to see before. Crying out in delight, she ran toward the house to tell Rowan of her discovery. When she saw a small, green pinecone sitting on the doorstep, she smiled, certain that it was a parting gift from the tree she loved.

Into the Fog

TWO WEEKS, GRACE THOUGHT TO HERSELF AS SHE STARED into the empty mug on her lap. *It's been two weeks since Rowan went off to college.* How breathless she had been lugging her daughter's suitcase up to the dorm room, how ill prepared she was for the final goodbye, how odd she'd felt driving out of the campus parking lot. She had gone back to the hotel and climbed into bed, exhausted by conflicting emotions of relief, pride, sadness, and ambivalence. After successfully raising two daughters and surviving menopause, what was left? And where was the fanfare, the gold medal, the crystal goblet of champagne?

Back at home, she rearranged the furniture. Realizing how little she cared about cooking, she ate popcorn and apples for dinner. She danced alone in the living room and stayed up late reading from her books of poetry. *At last, I can be the queen of my own castle.* She guarded her solitude like a jealous lover, knowing full well that her daughters would return over the holidays, filling the house with friends and music, but also leaving wet towels on the ground and dirty dishes in the sink.

Sunlight poured like honey through the front window on a warm autumn afternoon, as Grace sat reading on the couch. Deciding it was too fine a day to spend inside, she got in the car and drove through the wheat-colored hills near her home, with the windows open wide to hear the cicadas. She was headed to her favorite hiking trail high on the mountainside where she could watch the sun set over the Pacific Ocean. As she climbed the twisty mountain road, she noticed wispy patches of fog gathering, like tufts of wool snagged on a wire fence. By the time she parked her car, a thin gray blanket of mist had materialized around her, and the air temperature was noticeably cooler. The ground beneath her feet was parched, the stalks of teasel and fennel along the path were dry and dusty. The fog was moving in quickly, swallowing up the rocks and trees and hills around her. *How quickly things change.*

As she climbed the trail, pearly dew collected on spiderwebs and soggy thistledown. The thick gray mist distorted her senses and depth perception so much that she almost didn't recognize the magnificent buckeye tree that marked the halfway point on the trail. In springtime it was filled with bees swarming in its creamy blossom clusters; now it stood leafless and stark, preparing to drop its knobby fruits. *How quickly things change, how swiftly the familiar suddenly becomes unfamiliar.*

Up on the ridge, a stand of eucalyptus trees creaked and groaned in the wind. Feeling invigorated by the pungent, medicinal scent of the leaves, Grace continued up the fire trail, though her eyes were playing tricks on her. It seemed that she was entering into a mystical realm. Tree branches formed a vaulted archway overhead as she walked up what appeared to be the nave of a vast cathedral toward a shrouded figure who was waiting at the altar. A long forgotten wildness leapt in her heart, and she remembered what it felt like to be fearlessly alive. Her senses heightened, she stepped forward only to find herself standing by a lightning-blasted tree trunk. *What next?*

Another breath. Another step into the unknown where nothing was as it seemed, nothing was certain. There would be no sunset view, no "happy ending." What she did know was that beyond the fog, the cosmic rhythms were eternal: the moon cycling silently through its many faces, the tides in their endless dance, the sun and stars progressing from east to west across the sky, all reflecting back to her that Nature was her nature.

Glossary of Deities

With profound gratitude for the power and the wisdom of sacred archetypes, I offer these brief descriptions. May you find resonance, inspiration, and refreshment in these healing energies.

Aphrodite, Greek (Venus, Roman), goddess of beauty, love, and fertility

Artemis, maiden goddess of the moon, the hunt, protector of females and the natural world. Known for her independent nature

Cel Ati, Etruscan earth goddess

Changing Woman, goddess sacred to the Diné people, who changes continuously but never dies

Demeter, Greek goddess of the earth and of the harvest

Etain, Celtic goddess known as the Shining One, a shapeshifter associated with holy wells, trees, the sea, birds, healing, and transformation

Freya, Norse goddess of love, beauty, magic

Green Tara, Tibetan Buddhist deity who is the embodiment of compassion, action, and protection from fear and ignorance

Guabancex, Storm deity of the ancient Taino people, also known as Lady of the Winds

Hecate (Diana Trivia), Roman goddess of the crossroads, the triple goddess

Hestia, Greek goddess of the hearth and domesticity, whose sacred fire never went out

Kali, Hindu deva of creation, destruction, and preservation

La Loba, legendary Mexican wild woman/bone collector, associated with wolves

Mahuika, Maori fire deity

Mary Magdalene, Christian saint said to be a teacher, healer, and consort of Jesus Christ

Nephthys, Egyptian goddess of death and mourning, sister of Isis

Persephone, Greek goddess of the underworld, daughter of Demeter

Quan Yin, Chinese goddess/bodhisattva of compassion and mercy

Saule, Baltic solar deity; goddess of life, fertility, warmth, and health

Nuestra Virgen de Guadalupe, Mexican Catholic title of Blessed Virgin Mary, associated with motherhood, feminism, social justice

Yemanja, Yoruba Orisha, goddess of the living ocean, known as the mother of All

Green Man, ancient pagan archetype of the wild, compassionate masculine connected to the natural world, symbol of growth and rebirth

Acknowledgments

To Gaia: Mother, Mater, Matter.

In gratitude for the song of the bellbird, the bright pulse of starlight, the musings of the Brook Stream, the intoxication of Linden, steadfastness of Oak, the company of furbabies, and the largesse of Aotearoa.

Thank you to the mythical cast of characters and anam cara who made this book possible: St. Mary Ann, Sophia, Iona, my fairy godmother Fefe Fluffinwish; Karin, purveyor of firewater and sympathy; Alana, Alexandra, Anthony, Apollo, Bon Bon, Chiron, Chitvan, Claudi, Carolynne, Deirdre, Elana, Holly, Jade Lotus, Joy (my SOS); Leah Lamb, Ange and Scott, the legends of Lochmara; Lieza, Paru, Mary and Carlo at Sagrada Books; M.O.E., Sola Witt, Tine, Verena, Wild Bill and the Boys.

To Susan Griffin for her potent insights, editorial wizardry, and incomparable flair; Shannon Green for her wise counsel and kindhearted efficiency, the indefatigable Brooke Warner, and all the good people at SparkPress; the ebullient Fauzia Burke at FSB for making the ride so much fun!

Website and photo credit to the talented Paddy Sanders. *Grazie Mille!*

To women everywhere: *Plus et en vous.*

About the Author

Photo credit: Paddy Sanders

ELIZABETH GOULD has long been fascinated with feminine archetypes, mythology, and rites of passage. She has taught and mentored girls at puberty and is the former director of a nonprofit dedicated to positive menstrual/menopausal education. She holds a BA in Art History from Stanford University and an MS in Education from SUNY.

SELECTED TITLES FROM SPARKPRESS

SparkPress is an independent boutique publisher delivering high-quality, entertaining, and engaging content that enhances readers' lives, with a special focus on female-driven work. www.gosparkpress.com

Hindsight: A Novel, Mindy Tarquini. $16.95, 978-1-943006-01-4. A 33-year-old Chaucer professor who remembers all her past lives is desperate to change her future—because if she doesn't, she will never live the life of her dreams.

Squirrels in the Wall: A Novel, Henry Hitz. $16.95, 978-1-684630-22-6. In *Squirrels in the Wall*, humans and animals share heartbreak and ignorance about the nature of death. Together, they fashion a collage of a human family and its broader habitat, filled with dogs, cats, bees, turtles, squirrels, and mice, illuminating the tragicomic divide between humans and the natural world.

Goodbye, Lark Lovejoy: A Novel, Kris Clink, $16.95, 978-1-684630-73-8. A spontaneous offer on her house prompts grief-stricken Lark to retreat to her hometown, smack in the middle of the Texas Hill Country Wine Trail—but it will take more than a change of address to heal her broken family.

Charming Falls Apart: A Novel, Angela Terry, $16.95, 978-1-68463-049-3. After losing her job and fiancé the day before her thirty-fifth birthday, people-pleaser and rule-follower Allison James decides she needs someone to give her some new life rules—*and fast*. But when she embarks on a self-help mission, she realizes that her old life wasn't as perfect as she thought—and that she needs to start writing her own rules.

The Sea of Japan: A Novel, Keita Nagano. $16.95, 978-1-684630-12-7. When thirty-year-old Lindsey, an English teacher from Boston who's been as-signed to a tiny Japanese fishing town, is saved from drowning by a local young fisherman, she's drawn into a battle with a neighboring town that has high stakes for everyone—especially her.